MILADY'S ROOM

A Ghost Story

LENI REMEDIOS

ISBN: 9798631938632

To Su

It was nice to meet you
in Whitby

Leni Remelios

To Life

ACKNOWLEDGMENTS

I would like to take this opportunity to thank all the people who believed in *Milady's Room* from the very start and supported me during the whole realisation of this book. For a number of reasons, I cannot mention all of them here. I cannot fail to mention, though, my editor Mark Haywood - friend, editor and proof-reader - for his precious advice and honest feedback.

PREFACE

We are told by investigators that the majority of so-called 'ghostly apparitions' are characterized by a benign and harmless nature, if not one which is openly helpful in warning the living against negative influences and events.

Yet a small possibility of mischievous behaviour still has to be taken into account with regard to supernatural visits.

This story deals with this small possibility.

What we ask of the reader is to suspend any judgment and follow us in the reconstruction of the events contained in this story. We proudly describe ourselves as scrupulous and scientific researchers as well as respectful listeners.

Who are we to judge other people's feelings? Let alone those of ghosts.

Feelings rarely come in black and white. They more frequently come in a wide range of shades and quite often get entangled in such a way that one can hardly be distinguished from the other.

Ghosts, as far as we know, are not so very different from

us in this respect.

And if judging them isn't of any help, the only thing left to do is to listen to their stories: perhaps they will tell us something about ourselves.

BSPI
British Society for Psychical Investigation

INTRODUCTION

February 1902

Somewhere in Yorkshire, England

Lastsight Hill, the end of the route.

His bag was empty now, just one single letter left and someone up there was probably waiting for it. He lifted up his cap and wiped his forehead, all in a sweat despite the cold of February - the last bit of the hill was incredibly steep and he knew that he had to make this last effort every time, before going home. The end of the route - after that your day is finished, relief.

And yet there was always a bitter taste clinging to his throat when he was climbing up that hill and the mansion was unveiling itself from behind the tops of the trees. It wasn't just the physical effort and the steep uphill that made him sweat: it was the austere profile of the western tower, the splendid isolation the entire house was wrapped by, the unnerving sound of the wind howling all around it and making the heavy rusty gate creak. He couldn't help but smile to himself and think that perhaps his mother had read him too many eerie tales in front of the fireplace, when he was a child. But the huge gate was getting closer and the line of sweat was running down his temple, regardless.

He had the intention of ringing the bell, dropping the letter in the mailbox and rushing back immediately, as usual. No one had ever appeared in front of him so far and despite his curiosity he had never indulged himself to see who was coming to collect the posts. But this time he noticed that the figure of a young woman was among the roses, trimming them with long scissors. She noticed him as well. Meanwhile he realized that the whole area of the western lawns behind her was completely burnt out. She moved towards the gate, the long scissors still in her hands and a strange shadow over her eyes. As she stepped slowly towards him, he couldn't help but see that her face was crossed by deep scars. A big scar, in particular, crossed her left eye. Some wounds had dried but other ones could not have been very old, because he could still see a rather pink shade around the borders; not only the face, but also the arms were covered by scars - he could see them because she kept her sleeves rolled up above the elbows, for her gardening efforts. Lastly, with a shudder he detected a deep, strangle-like mark on her throat. His pale face probably proved to her that he was frightened because suddenly she stopped and dropped the scissors on the ground. Then she came closer to the gate, where he could see her more clearly. He was amazed by the uncanny contrast the scars made with her graceful face, by her long curly red hair moving in the wind and showing premature white flecks, by her deep green eyes: such beauty wasted by such cruelty. A few moments earlier he was on the point of running away miserably, frightened by her wounded face, the scissors and the gloomy mansion in the background…it was her odd kind of beauty that kept him rooted to the spot.

The post office of the little village of ****** was still open. The lazy, golden light of the afternoon entered through the glass door panels and an awareness of the final minutes of the working day gave people, workers and customers alike, a relaxed and peaceful frame of mind.

There were few customers: Mrs Wood, an elderly lady, who came there almost every day, sending "important letters" and cards to her relatives, so she said, probably just good excuses to have a chat with the staff; Mr Reede, the butcher, still with his blood-stained apron, always busy with some invoices; and finally a wealthy, good-looking, middle-aged man, with the silver chain of his pocket watch hanging clearly visible from his waistcoat pocket, smiling and talking amiably to the postmaster: he was Julius MacAllister, a solid Scottish man, with a permanent slight smile on his face under a thin, neat moustache. His wealth and his social position didn't keep him at all from mingling and chatting with villagers. On the contrary, he took a sort of delight in doing so. His lightly red skin revealed that he was the kind of man who doesn't disdain the pleasures of life - alcohol least of all - but knows his limits exactly and would never exceed them.

Mr Toulson, the old postmaster, was serving him, when Mr Reede, going towards the glass door, hesitated on seeing Peter, the young new mail man: he was coming in, his bag obviously empty as he was at the end of his route, his face curiously bewildered.

'It seems that our Peter has just seen a ghost!' said Mr Reede, laughing loudly.

The boy came in and everybody was looking at him, laughing. He stared for a moment at Mr Reede's blood-stained apron, then took his bag off and threw it on an empty chair, still maintaining his bewildered expression but visibly irritated by the laughter.

'Come on lad, what's happened to you? We'll have our tea now and whatever was the matter, it will pass off,' said Mr Toulson from behind the counter, looking at Peter now and then while counting MacAllister's letters. Mr Reede had stopped in the doorway, uncertain whether to leave or to stay.

'Oh, leave me alone. I'd feel ashamed if I told you that,' said Peter after having flung himself down on another spare chair. But as he kept his serious face, in spite of the hilarity in the post office at its closing time, Mr Toulson glanced at him in a puzzled way.

'Alright, I'll tell you,' sighed Peter after a few seconds silence, 'My last delivery, as you know, was for Lastsight Hill.'

On hearing this name MacAllister lifted his head.

'Poor lad,' a scratchy old voice was heard from behind the Scottish man, where Mrs Wood waited quietly in the queue. 'I'd be scared too if I was you, to be in the surroundings of that place.'

'Well, I was given just a few hints about it. Mr Toulson, while he was explaining the delivery route to me, told me that strange events happened over there, but nothing more. Today I had to go there and...oh, it's just silly.' And he hushed himself up, waving his hand.

'Tell us, young man, what scared you?'

This time the voice came from MacAllister himself, stern and firm. His letters were arranged and Mr Toulson was busy now with Mrs Wood. But it was difficult to keep the attention of the old lady on her "important letters", because it seemed that this time she didn't care for them at all: her attention was attracted by the conversation between the elegant middle-aged man, standing right in the middle of the office and the scruffy young lad, sitting lazily on his chair, his oversized uniform hanging oddly from his person.

'Mrs Wood...Mrs Wood!' repeated Mr Toulson in vain.

'I know the owners of that mansion very well,' said MacAllister suddenly.

'I know them too!' said the old lady. MacAllister turned towards her, as he had not realised she was behind him until that moment, and gave her an odd glance, 'Well, not directly,' she went on, 'but, who doesn't know what happened last year over there?'

Mr Toulson understood the situation. Shaking his head, he abandoned the counter and went to shut the glass-panelled door right in front of Mr Reede, who had realized that going away meant missing something.

'I'll prepare the tea,' Mr Toulson murmured, going towards the back office, a room separated from the rest of the shop by a low wooden wall.

'Well, I'm not local, Mrs Wood,' Peter replied. 'I don't know anything about the town's stories and to tell you the truth I was never interested in gossip.'

MacAllister remained standing looking at the young man, his perennial smile on his face, opening and closing his eyelids like a big cat staring at the sunlight.

Mr Toulson, troubled with cups and teapot, and presenting his back to the party, said loudly, 'Why don't you all take a seat?'

At his words Mrs Wood immediately obeyed, hurrying with fast little steps towards the nearest seat, dragging her wooden stick noisily, leaning it against the wall and finally sitting down with a satisfied smile on her face.

MacAllister moved slowly to the seat opposite Peter, drew out his pipe and, after having obtained a sign of approval by the postmaster, lit it and began to smoke, quietly expecting something more from the young mailman. Peter stared at him and sank back in his chair, his hair in a mess, his eyes still bewildered.

For a long while he kept silent. Then he started to report confidently and loudly about how it was a day like all the other days and how he had simply been climbing the road to Lastsight Hill as he normally did at the end of his route, cautious throughout about revealing his real, fearful feelings. But then, when the moment came to talk about the charming scarred lady, his tone changed curiously: he lowered his eyes to the floor and started to talk quietly, almost in a whisper, almost in a trance.

MacAllister's cat eyes narrowed with interest behind the smoking clouds of his pipe. Mrs Wood bent forward in her chair, trying to catch his words. She was nodding energetically at every sentence, smiling and turning her head agitatedly from the Scottish man to the lad and back again, like a ferret. Finally Mr Toulson joined the party, carrying a tray full of teacups and biscuits.

'Oh, that's very kind of you!' exclaimed the ferret lady. 'Did she say something to you?' she asked suddenly, turning to Peter.

'No,' he sighed, 'she just took the letter from my hands, looked at it attentively and then, with half a smile – a sad smile – lifted her eyes and said "Thank you". That's all.'

The old lady looked disappointed. She was expecting something more to fill her afternoon.

'If you know them well, can you explain to me why they keep such sinister servants?'

Peter's question was obviously directed to MacAllister.

'She's not a servant,' he answered after a puff of smoke. 'She's the mistress of the house and I am one of her employees.'

Peter was visibly shocked by the news. He wasn't worried that he might have offended the man and his mistress: he knew MacAllister was a good-tempered man, who did not care at all about formalities.

And yet, now Peter was curious, eagerly curious: yes, the Peter who disliked gossip wanted to know something more.

'Well,' went on MacAllister, 'it would be rather more correct to say that she's the only one managing the house. When I told you "I know them" I said it unconsciously. Maybe because I have not yet accepted the idea of his death.' He exchanged a glance with the postmaster, who obviously knew everything about everyone. 'I mean, the master of the house.'

'Why are you looking at each other in that way? What on earth happened in that mansion? And what about her?'

'One question at time, young man!' exclaimed the old ferret lady with alarm, worried that the fury of youth could be irksome to the elegant, good-mannered gentleman.

'Never mind, madam,' the latter said calmly, 'I completely understand the fascination and the bewilderment a place like Lastsight Hill and its residents arouses in a stranger.'

He stared at Peter firmly.

'Do you really want to know the story of that woman and her husband, Lord K? Well, I warn you that you had better not be in a hurry - it will take a long time.'

At these words Mrs Wood patted the little cushion lying at the back of her seat.

Peter sat up better on his chair, bending his back forward, an eager look in his eyes.

'All right, I'm ready.'

'Weren't you the one who didn't care about anyone and anything?' asked Mr Toulson, amused.

But Peter didn't look at him, nor did he answer. He just hung on MacAllister's lips.

CHAPTER ONE

MARY ANN'S COTTAGE

'I will begin at a tiny cottage here in the village: the abode of Mrs Ashby.

Mary Ann Kavanagh, widow Ashby, lived with her elder daughters Daphne and Page, her twelve year old son Donovan and the housekeeper, Gertrude, in a little cottage that lay at the corner of the main road, swathed in greenery. A front veranda looked onto lawns full of roses and ornamental plants of every kind, while the rear garden enjoyed the scents and the colours of many homegrown vegetables, at the side of which the washing hung constantly from the lines. The lawns at the front were crossed by a path made with stepping stones from the local brook. It linked the little wooden gate to the house entrance, but was unfinished and the last pebbles set down on the path forced any visitors to lengthen their stride towards the doorstep, in order to avoid contact with the muddy turf in between. Beyond the gate a few little steps led directly to the main road of ******. The cottage and the garden were spared the curiosity of passers-by thanks to a little wall and a tall myrtle shrub.

Indoors it was humble and cosy. Some portraits hung on the wall; the heavy furniture in elegant carved mahogany and evidently well selected upholstery gave a hint of nobility that couldn't escape visitors' eyes. Any awe inspired by such nobility was instantly mitigated by the warm colours of the upholstery itself, by the tea service that lay clearly visible in the cupboard, decorated in the refined local style, and by the upright piano which, right in the main room of the cottage, was an open invitation to conviviality: in a place like this it was impossible not to feel at ease.

Mary Ann's husband, Joseph Ashby, had died eight years earlier; he was the last descendant of a once noble landowners' family. Alcohol had devoured his liver, but had also dissipated his last possessions, leaving Mary Ann a widow, in weak financial conditions, with three children to rear, a house to keep and in almost complete isolation: her own surviving relatives were all in Ireland and her husband's family had never approved of his marriage to an Irish woman who had once been a servant, ascribing the reason for his turning to drink directly to her. When he died, they made it their business not to support the widow and her children; on the other hand, Mary Ann didn't weaken her immense pride with any request for help.

She had always been hard tempered and indefatigable: she rolled up her sleeves, first selling their last remaining lands - with which she covered her husband's most urgent debts - then devising many little expediencies. In doing so, she had guaranteed her own family a dignified life, even if the comforts and the habits of their previous social condition were definitely lost.

Of all the possessions they once had, just a little plot remained - where they grew vegetables to sell at the local market - and the cottage itself. They used the little rear garden of the house to its best advantage for their own subsistence and Mary Ann had been teaching sewing and dressmaking skills to her girls, in order to gain some more money: she passed to them all the secrets and abilities which had been inherited for generations and which she herself had partially used while working as a servant.

As regards to their father's death, the only consolation was that they were young when it happened, too young to get used to luxury in a permanent way. So they accepted the change with difficulty at first, but then their flexible children's minds adapted themselves to the conditions of their new life. Harvesting the garden was simply a new amusement and the girls sewed skirts and gowns as they did for their dolls' clothes. Mary Ann was particularly able in guiding them through the transition: having known both sides of the coin, she didn't find herself in a panic at what had been the most critical moment in her family's life, as would undoubtedly have occurred to a lady born of high rank. And once the hardest period had been overcome, once they no longer had to hide at the creditors' knocks or resign themselves to having just onion soup for dinner, we can say they led a life characterized by happiness, in a state of mind in which they fulfilled their real needs and didn't indulge in luxuries.

Daphne, the elder daughter, was now two and twenty and her face showed all the typical features of the Ashby family: blond hair - just shaded with a nuance of red — extraordinarily pale skin and light blue eyes. She was good tempered, always calm and amiable, and in accomplishing housework duties she was in perfect harmony with her mother, doing whatever she was told to do without complaint. She could never be heard speaking ill of someone else. Not because she was hypocritical, but because she was kind, genuinely kind, the dangerous type of kindness that could move some people to abuse her feelings.

Page, the youngest daughter, nineteen years old, was of the opposite temper and her appearance clearly showed it: her long, red wavy hair and her freckles, that flew gently across her face, revealed a pride that ran back directly to her mother's Irish roots. She used to accomplish her housework duties with a humble attitude and a spirit of sacrifice, but she could no longer find – like her sister did – any kind of pleasure in the sewing duties she had to perform, nor in gossiping about the villagers or the notable local families, an occupation that was keeping her mother's and her sister's minds busy during the housework. Once her duties were accomplished, she went alone to the little library of the cottage – she had fought resolutely with her mother to keep her from selling all the books in there – and flung herself in a chair to read one of the volumes; or else she took her little notebook and pencil and got away from the house, directing herself towards the moors: as usual, she would seek a quiet place under a tree or by the bank of a brook, contemplating in the distance the massive, oddly shaped rocks scattered on the fields and on the hills, giant crumbling witnesses of a past that traced itself back maybe to millions of years earlier, she loved to think.

She curiously synthesized the impulsive temper of her Irish mother and the introspection of her English father, who in his sober hours used to dedicate his time to the numerous volumes in his library.

Twelve year old Donovan was a very perspicacious fellow

for his age. For the moment his role was to counterbalance, with his lively adolescent spark, a predominantly female family.

He used to ramble around silently with the weightlessness of an elf. And, yes, he was the one who was building up the paved path on the front lawns, choosing carefully one at the time the best pebbles and stones that were lying by the local brook.

Finally there was Gertrude, the stern but amiable housekeeper, recently arrived from Hamburg. She gave a significant contribution to the domestic life, as well as to the education, of the three children who, from the youngest age, were introduced to the study of the German language.

In all honesty, Donovan was not the only one to break the Ashby female axis: there were also the visits paid by Mr Rudolf Bachmeier, a retired attorney, who had taken Mary Ann's situation to heart and since poor Joseph's death had tried to help her by any means possible in the management of her scarce family finances.

Born in Hamburg as well, it was he that found and recommended Gertrude to Mary Ann, after she had to get rid of all the servants.

"Gertrude does for three," he assured her. And he was right: she was a housekeeper, a maid, a tutor. She was not young anymore, but had a stout constitution and accomplished all her housework with the highest sense of duty; she even got irritated whenever Mary Ann invited her to have a rest. From the everyday cleaning to harvesting vegetables, from trimming roses to wringing a chicken's neck, she never evaded anything and while doing her housework she could even save up some energy to correct the children's pronunciation of some German words. Despite her constant stern appearance, they soon got attached to her: she became, from the beginning, a member of the family and would never have left the Ashbys for any reason in the world.

The precious introduction of Gertrude into the family was one of the reasons why Mary Ann felt she had to be forever grateful towards Bachmeier.

Actually Bachmeier got in touch with the Ashbys thanks to the bad habit he shared with the dead Joseph: it had never affected him in such a dramatic way as it had his friend, but we have to admit he never completely lost his predilection for the bottle. There were rumours that he had asked for premature retirement, just because he had been threatened to be expelled from the Bar, due to his habit. Unmarried, and with no important occupations during the day, he left the noisy town where he practiced to move to the quiet village of ******, choosing a little lodging at the foot of a hill to end his days as a bachelor. From that moment onwards he had refused to keep any kind of alcohol – so he said – maintaining his habit just for the few hours he spent in the club, where I met him. From the beginning I understood he had once been a very clever and skilled fellow, with a rigour typical of a German mind, but his attachment to certain pleasures of life had made him digress from his path, until it had ruined his career. I was particularly struck by his humour, accompanied by a peculiar acumen that alcohol couldn't have destroyed yet. Some of his jokes and comments arrived when you didn't expect them at all, like sharp little arrows shot at a prey after a long and unseen watch by its predator. And they were always to the point. With time he became more and more present in the Ashbys' life, offering his help in exchange for hot meals now and then.

Page could scarcely bear his presence and she concealed her personal dislike of him with difficulty, even if she never uttered a word to that effect, neither to her mother nor directly to him. By contrast, Daphne's pure and kind soul considered him "a gentle and amusing man" - so she defined him - which irritated Page even further, incapable as she was of understanding how such a refined mind as Bachmeier's could become wasted by alcohol in such a futile way.

She evidently was too young to know anything about human weaknesses - notwithstanding her indirect experience with her father - and how swiftly and easily a human soul, albeit the cleverest and sharpest it could be, could surprisingly slip on the slope of vices and addictions. As with any other woman of her age with unmarried adult daughters, Mary Ann's most urgent worry was to find a good match for them, in particular for the eldest - Daphne would be three and twenty in May and as time passed Mary Ann grew increasingly worried about her daughter's destiny. Everyone in the surroundings knew their situation and it came as no surprise that the local young men were very careful not to offer a marriage proposal to Daphne Ashby, even though she was so pretty as to undoubtedly capture their attention. But marrying Daphne Ashby meant marrying her family's problems; her Irish component, for many protestant English families, was a further reason to deter them from any plan of marriage with their precious offspring and it even provided an opportunity for sarcastic remarks, when the doings of the Ashby women were served on the silver plate of tea time gossip.

Among them a theme quite often recurred: Mary Ann was not at all inclined to give her consent to a marriage with a low-class man, and occasions like that were not lacking. Her notorious pride kept her from taking such a decision: the memory of her own family's sacrifices – their emigration after the potato famine when she was just a child, her hard work with her parents in the fields and then as a maid in noble English mansions – was still vivid in her mind and, as she had touched the comforts and prosperities of a wealthy life, the mere idea of marrying Daphne to a worker or to a local shopkeeper's son was tantamount to a degrading defeat.

That's why Daphne Ashby – so the young rich ladies used to murmur in their parlours - was doomed to remain unmarried until the end of her life.

But something new happened on an evening just like this, with exactly the same tender sunbeams entering softly through the large windows of the cottage.

Mr Bachmeier was the ambassador of information which would change their lives forever.

He knocked gently at the entrance door and as soon as Gertrude opened it he entered with a face gayer than usual. "Guten Abend! My dear Mrs Ashby, what is this expression I see on your face?"

Mary Ann shook her head.

"Haven't you seen it? The new shop in the centre of the village."

"You mean Mr Allan's clothes shop? It's very nice indeed, but what's the matter?"

"What's the matter?" she exclaimed alarmed. "All the young women pop into it as if bewitched and spend all their families' money in there. All the new fashion from London, sometimes from Paris, they say. Can't you understand what it all means for us now? We could already feel a slight decrease in commissions in the last few weeks; not that I didn't expect so, sooner or later - I'm not a fool: new textile factories are emerging all across the country and not just since yesterday. But you always hope that…oh, let's stop there, it will be our ruin anyway."

Bachmeier kept his smile on his face, almost irreverently.

There were a few seconds silence between them and a scolding glance in Mary Ann's and Gertrude's eyes. Daphne gazed at them sadly from the sofa where she was sewing and Page slowly moved closer. How could he dare show no tact on hearing this sad news?

"Well, Mrs Ashby, I'm here to announce something that will surely make you forget your troubles of the moment and in all likelihood will affect your very future."

Mary Ann lost her scolding attitude and grew puzzled.

"What are you talking about, by all the saints?"

"Take a seat madam, I'm afraid you will be overwhelmed by emotion," he giggled, amused. "You and all your family are invited to the next Lady Deville Charity Ball."

Mary Ann clapped her hands over her mouth and looked excitedly at Daphne, who jumped for joy from her seat.

"Wait wait, that's just the beginning: guess where it will be held?"

They looked at each other, but nobody could guess it - they had not been invited to a ball for a long time and they had no idea where noble families presently met to amuse themselves. Page stepped back with the intention of seeking refuge for herself in the library: the prospect of a ball was not at all attractive to her. Staring into Mary Ann's eyes Bachmeier said aloud,

"Lastsight Hill.'"

'Lastsight Hill?!' The sudden exclamation instantaneously broke the magical atmosphere that had been created in the post office. 'I can't believe a ball was held over there! Such a gaunt and solitary place.' Peter had moved suddenly in his chair on hearing that.

'It's exactly the same reaction the Ashbys had,' nodded MacAllister. 'You've seen it: it's certainly not a place to suggest a perfect spot for a ball,' he said with a stifled laugh.

'My nieces told me it was one of the most beautiful balls they had ever taken part in,' said Mrs Wood suddenly. 'Such a magnificent hall, with marvelous tapestries and so finely furnished.' Her eyes were almost shedding tears remembering the words of her nieces, as if she herself had been at this legendary ball. Slowly her smile faded and she lifted her finger as if to point out an important subject – 'But they also told me a rather queer particular about it…'

'Please, please Mrs Wood,' MacAllister interrupted her. 'Pardon me if I appear rude, but it would be better not to anticipate any particulars of this story.'

The old lady nodded obediently and MacAllister went on solemnly.

"'Oh that is very exciting news," answered Mary Ann, "but, tell me, with all the beautiful spots we have here, why has Lady Deville chosen Lastsight Hill?"

"Well, maybe you know that it's a long-standing custom for the Devilles always to choose a different spot for their annual Charity Ball," Bachmeier went on pompously. "This year she was invited directly by Lord K to hold her event in his mansion, Lastsight Hill."

"You mean *Lostsoul* Hill!" the lively voice of Donovan, until now unseen, erupted from the end of the room. Everybody had got too involved with the novelty of the ball to have noticed him approaching from the front garden after taking out from under his shirt a stone from the brook and laying it on the unfinished path. He had entered the room light of foot and silent as a snake and had caught the conversation in the middle.

"Donovan, please!" his mother reproached him.

"Everybody calls it that!" He glanced with a smile at Page who, on hearing about the strange setting of the ball, had been restrained by curiosity and instead of collapsing in one of the library's chairs, had remained on the threshold to listen. She smiled back at her brother, suffocating her laugh: they didn't speak very much to each other, but there was a kind of complicity between them that came out at particular moments, as though Page was not an adult, but a twelve year old boy like Donovan.

"The boy is right," said Bachmeier. "The nickname that has stuck to Lord K's estate is indeed not inappropriate." He stopped for a moment, not knowing exactly what they might know about the master of that house.

"If you think so, it puzzles me why he would give a ball in his mansion," exclaimed Mary Ann more curious than ever. "It's true that very odd things are murmured about him. Since he moved here nobody has ever met him. We don't even know his family name or how he looks. The only thing that is confirmed is that he's still deeply afflicted by his wife's death, that's why he moved here from Eastern Europe, isn't it?"

"Exactly," nodded Bachmeier. "Furthermore, together with his wife he lost his first-born. The child died right at the moment when his mother gave him birth. And that's why he prefers to conduct a very solitary life." He said that with a plain tone of the voice, as if he was talking about Mister Allan's new shop or about last year's crop.

A sudden shadow crossed Mary Ann's eyes, as if an invisible yet vulnerable chord had been touched inside her. "He suffers a grief that very few people could fully understand," he went on, apologetically, in a lower voice.

"They say he brought his wife's corpse with him and buried it among the plants in his glasshouse!" exclaimed Donovan with hilarity, with the irreverence typical of his age.

"Donovan!" - this time it was Page herself who reproached her brother: she had turned again into a nineteen year old lady. "Don't go beyond the limit."

"But it's true, I heard the Wilson brothers talking in that

21

way!"

"Oh, very reliable indeed," answered Page sarcastically. "They are just spoiled children, so bored that they have nothing better to do than invent legends about neighbours!"

"Well said, little Page," burst out Bachmeier.

"I'm not little," she murmured.

"Well, the truth is that everything is getting more and more obscure," Mary Ann cut in. "I mean, why on earth should a person like him, after having deliberately chosen a solitary life, with such grief in his heart, suddenly decide to host a ball in his own house?"

Bachmeier laughed. "You know, Mrs Ashby, this is one of those occasions in which informal acquaintances and casual speech can be very precious in one's life. It happens that I have intelligence of an ulterior purpose to this ball, something that very few people know, and me among them." He took a long puff from his cigar, keeping them waiting in curiosity.

"He's looking for a wife."

"Oh!" exclaimed Mary Ann, her hands clasped to her face. She had turned automatically towards Daphne, who looked surprised and indeed quite embarrassed.

"I got it from the club today," went on Bachmeier. "You know I go there sometimes," (that is not true: I know he goes there *every* day). "I was setting off when I was stopped by MacAllister, Lord K's attendant. He told me that deliberately, knowing that I'm one of your closest acquaintances and that you have daughters."

"But pardon me, sir, it's very kind of you to think that this event would be a great opportunity for our Daphne, and indeed it is, but ****** and the surroundings are full of very pretty rich ladies. Daphne is very pretty, it's true, but how could you be so self-confident as to insinuate that she should have more chance with him than the others? You know our situation very well and I suppose Mr MacAllister does as well." Daphne sat back slowly on her seat, looking at Bachmeier. But before he could say anything in answer, Page stepped forward and said abruptly,

"Mother is right, are you mocking us?"

"Page, I didn't mean that!" Mary Ann scolded her.

"So what, Mother? We are talking about taking part in a charity ball, while we don't even have the money to buy material for new clothes, as work has been slow recently, hasn't it? Isn't it rather that we are invited because *we* are the object of the charity?"

Bachmeier persevered with a smile, while Mary Ann and Daphne tried to hush Page. Donovan's muffled laughs were audible from the carpet on which he sat.

"Well, what you said sounds quite wise and prudent, but you didn't let me finish, my dear young lady: I will correct myself by saying that Lord K *needs* a wife, for a specific reason that I will explain. He is undoubtedly rich, but his eccentric way of life and his gloomy mansion are not at all attractive to the local rich young ladies - with their connections they can easily aim at a better choice. Furthermore, don't forget he's a stranger and his eastern accent, I am told, is strong enough to make him less attractive, even if his knowledge of the English language is almost perfect. Ah, I learnt that from my personal experience!" He laughed a bitter, hearty laugh.

"Who told you? They say nobody met him," pointed out Page.

"I told you I have precious acquaintances," Bachmeier smiled to her in a defiant attitude.

"And anyway, the point is: he's rich, he's in need of a wife, but none of our upper-class ladies would willingly marry him. Do you still think this is not a good opportunity for

Daphne?"

Mary Ann again clapped her hands and smiled decisively: she was conquered. Bachmeier's arguments seemed to have sense. Furthermore, she could face her family's future with less distressing thoughts. At least she could hope for something.

"What about his reasons for needing a wife, as you said?" asked Page, drawing everyone back to reality.

"Well, it's a long story. In short, his father-in-law has claimed back his daughter's possessions."

"Oh, that is very disrespectful indeed!" Mary Ann exclaimed. "Some people don't care about the dead at all, nor about bereavement nor relatives still in mourning."

"Wait Mary Ann, it's more complex than you think. I should explain a little more," he paused to get a puff from his cigar and went on even more pompously. "I have to say first of all that Lord K's life has been cruelly crossed by death, more than once. He married his wife in the weirdest situation you can imagine - they married furtively, as Lady Lavinia's father – this was her name – had never liked him. But this is nothing, many marriages were made against parents' consent." Again Mary Ann lowered her eyes.

"The oddest thing is that they married soon after a tragic event in which three members of Lady Lavinia's family had been found horribly slaughtered. Well, they had just discovered the three corpses and…what a perfect opportunity to get married, don't you think? Taking advantage of the confusion of the moment they ran to the local church with two passers-by as witnesses, still with their blood-stained clothes, and that's it."[1]

Everyone remained in silence.

---

[1] See Leni Remedios, *The Discomfort Zone* (unpublished novel), the prequel to *Milady's Room*.

"This is the strangest marriage I ever heard about," Mary Ann said and began to think that maybe Lord K wasn't such a good match for her daughter.

"Don't think that, madam," Bachmeier had guessed her thoughts. "Lord K and Lady Lavinia didn't do this without any concern towards their relatives. On the contrary, they were the only ones to really care for them and did everything in their power to prevent what happened. One of the murdered was Lavinia's younger sister, Lord K's patient – you know he's a doctor, don't you? – and I am told he took the case of the poor girl particularly to his heart. That's why his father-in-law hates him so much: he is an unscrupulous rich man, for whom the most important thing is his own honour. I won't explain how all this happened but, even if not materially, for many reasons we can say *he* was the one really responsible for the three horrible deaths."

"This is really loathsome about that man," Mary Ann nodded, "but how can he have claim to his daughter's possession? Is he allowed?"

"Lord K's father-in-law is one of the most powerful notables among the local wealthy Polish society and once he decides on something, he gets it," said Bachmeier with another puff of smoke.

"And is it certain that another marriage can prevent him from doing so?" asked Page doubtfully.

"Yes, a marriage and the mere possibility of an heir would prevent him from any claim."

"Oh, I see," exclaimed Mary Ann.

"Well, I've told you everything." Bachmeier got up and moved towards the door.

"I only forgot to tell you that the ball will be held in two weeks."

"Two weeks?" Exclaimed the ladies with one voice.

"We have to make a new gown for ourselves, darlings, we have nothing decent to go to a ball!" Mary Ann began to pace to and fro frenetically.

Bachmeier left them with a satisfied smile, while inside the cottage the paroxysm of excitement for the new event was just at its beginning.'

CHAPTER TWO

THE MOVE

'Deep-hearted man, express
Grief for thy Dead in silence like to death--
Most like a monumental statue set
In everlasting watch and moveless woe
Till itself crumble to the dust beneath.
Touch it; the marble eyelids are not wet:
If it could weep, it could arise and go'

From *Grief*, Elizabeth Barrett Browning

'You shouldn't imagine that the idea of the ball came from
Lord K's own mind. Poor fellow…'
Just as a black cloud, passing before the sun, obscures a

luxurious wood below, in the same way the perennial smile worn by MacAllister faded, his hand suspended in the air holding the pipe, his eyes lost somewhere, as if preparing to be filled by silent tears. They revealed that Lord K was more than a master. But the tears would not fall. MacAllister knew how to control himself.

'His soul was doomed to woe and torment. Any suggestion of cheerfulness was inevitably hateful to him. But it's time for me to take a step back and introduce you to his story and how he arrived here.'

He recovered abruptly with a quick movement of his head; his eyes came back promptly to the post office room and eventually, to allow himself a little time, he drew another puff of smoke.

'You already know something about his life in Krakow and about his weird marriage with Lady Lavinia. Moreover, you already know that she died giving birth to her first born and the baby didn't survive either. It was a tragedy; no human word would ever be able to explain it. What an absurdity that Death is so close at hand in the biggest celebration of Life. And yet it still happens so frequently.

Can you imagine how a human soul could bear such an affliction? An unspeakable grief, that's what it is. It's in moments like these that a mind seriously runs the risk of taking the path of insanity. Only a tremendous effort of will together with the rudder of rationality can avoid it. He did the cleverest thing he could do, from my personal point of view: he decided to cut himself off completely from his past, going away from the people and places that would have bothered and disturbed him. But in reality, he didn't want to escape in order to begin a new life and he wasn't resolved on an oblivion of sorrow: he simply cut out from his past the shape of his wife and carried it with him. And that is the part of his decision that I find less clever: I've witnessed over time how it has dragged him down the slope of morbidity. He just wanted to find a lair in which he could silently consume his own grief, undisturbed, secluded from society. Alone, just with the remembrance of his beloved for companionship. If he were not the smart fellow I know him to be, he surely would have taken his own life. But he used to tell me that to die was not up to him, that he had no right to decide upon it. What can you say about those wise words? Uttered by someone who had seen the lives of his loved ones taken by destiny with blind cruelty? On the other hand, he considered himself already dead inside and went on leading his life accordingly.

Going back to the narrative: he conducted an investigation through his agents and it came to his knowledge that a neglected building lay on the top of a hill in a faraway land. It was drawn to his attention cursorily, among many other beautiful properties that his agents considered more suitable to his wealthy position. But the appearance of this shabby building in a faded picture struck him at once - it was an old medieval castle of which just a tower and a few battlements remained on the west side. In 1871 an eccentric aristocrat, Lord Coventry, bought the estate for a ridiculous amount and together with his friend, the architect John Reilly, built a mansion that kept the original ruins of the castle, adding a wing that followed the aesthetic standards of the day. The result was a quite singular building, half medieval, half modern. Inside it was structured in a very complex way, but a detail in particular was rather curious: naturally there was an impressive central hall with a massive staircase, as in all mansions like that, but then there were another two different staircases to reach the upstairs bedrooms, one more sober for the gentlemen on the west wing, one sumptuous for the ladies on the east wing. At the time British architects wanted to exhibit their own conformity to the values dear to our Victorian society, according to which any risk of promiscuity had to be eliminated - the idea of the two sets of stairs therefore followed this model. I wouldn't swear though that Lord Coventry and his friend, nonconformist as they were, intended to honour these values when they built Lastsight Hill mansion.   On the contrary, their irreverence was such that they deliberately decided to use the different staircases as a trick during their extravagant balls and parties. So the original plan was turned ironically to its opposite. Many legends circulated about their parties and nobody knows what is really true about them. The only certain thing we know from the servants is that those staircases weren't used to keep men separate from women, but rather to generate confusion between them and you can only imagine what happened by a certain point of the night, when the excitement of the party had grown higher. Anyway, it was the destiny of that place to return again to neglect - Lord Coventry's extravagances led him to ruin. His incredible parties had all the oddest attractions you can figure: singers and musicians from France and Italy were invited, exotic animals were parading on the lawns for the pleasure of his guests, plants from all over the world enriched his magnificent glasshouse…it couldn't last forever, not even for the richest man on earth. Lastsight Hill was once again doomed to decay. Lord Coventry left the estate, cursed by his creditors; no one ever knew where exactly he had escaped to.

Ivy soon began to climb up the walls, inexorable, fast, as though it was the real owner of the building, reclaiming its property with eager satisfaction. The mansion - a house that had always echoed to the voices of hundreds of people attracted by the reputation of Lord Coventry's legendary parties - went back to the silence of the surrounding moors, like a child that humbly returns to his mother's arms after having been naughty.

And it was *that* face of Lastsight Hill that Lord K was attracted to: the silent naughty child among his mother's arms, the moors. What better place to hide his misery than this? What better place to lead a misanthropist's life?

He had planned his journey to England with obsessive precision. He'd refused any privilege and had reached the German shores by means of a shared coach, followed by a plain cart conveying his trunk. The latter was strictly guarded by his loyal valet Cezary, who had always been deeply attached to Lord K and to Lady Lavinia (he considered them his own real family) and would have followed his master anywhere. From Germany Lord K moved to England by steamboat - a crowded, low class one, in what was to be his last immersion into human society.

With a masochistic irony, he had planned to land in Whitby, where the well-known fictional character of Count Dracula had landed on his arrival from Transylvania. You may be induced to smile at his extravagance. Yes, indeed: it was a queer idea born from an ill-minded, desperate man who considered himself a living corpse. But his intention was opposite to that of the fictional character. He didn't at all want to perpetuate his own kind - he just wanted to be neglected, hoping that the rest of society would soon forget about him and ultimately hoping to die prematurely and to reach his beloved.

He stopped for one night in Whitby, taking the occasion to visit the town. If you ever have visited it you would certainly know the feeling aroused by the impressive sight of the cliff, so well described by the Irish novelist, with the ruins of the abbey and the jagged old gravestone profiles outlined against the sky, the wild sea roaring underneath.

He walked up the slope, stopping at the top of the hill, among the stones of the graveyard, consumed by the agents of time and weather. I'm ready to guess that, looking down at the sea from that evocative spot, a bad thought came across his mind: the creeping temptation of crossing the line and letting himself go. Human beings are weak and sometimes it doesn't take much for one to take tough decisions that rationally they would never take. But, as I told you, he was a clever man and for his sake his rationality got the better of his negative feelings.

I will never forget – how can I? – the first time I met him. My role, as estate agent, was to introduce him to the property and to explain accurately every detail, that was all. He descended from his carriage: a tall, dark-dressed man, with long black hair and dried hollow eyes that – it was evident – had no more tears to shed. Deep furrows lined his brow and his lips were constantly tightened. Beyond his melancholy he had a sort of magnetism and the manners of an Eastern European man, so straightforward and self-confident, disarmed my British formality. After having shown him all the recesses of the house, I was about to leave him and to go back home when, unexpectedly, he turned to me and asked, with his strong accent, *"Will you work for me?"* And that's how I became one of his attendants.'

'So you left your job abruptly, without having enquired first who your new employer was?' asked Mrs Wood incredulously, her blue eyes expanding.

'At once,' answered MacAllister, without concealing a certain pride.

'Sometimes people take important decisions led only by a strong intuition or feeling, with no tangible proof about whether what they are going to do would be good or not. Most of the time these are the best decisions.'

'Oh,' Mrs Wood leaned back onto her chair, not entirely convinced by his explanation.

'Briefly,' he resumed, 'Lastsight Hill, once the spot of the most crowded and gayest parties, was now guardian of a solitary, desperate mourning. It was pitiful to me to see how his sorrow was gradually drying up all the remains of humanity left in his soul. As I had foreseen, he was growing grumpy, brusque and when he was not in this mood he was wrapped up in his silent melancholy. To me it was like perceiving a spectre.

My master's days were dreary and methodical - he was observing a systematic, obstinate bereavement, wearing all the time a strange collection of medieval-like, buckles-crossed black suits. He wore them like a sort of uniform and he never used other garments, except for a long black hooded cloak during wet days. Early in the morning he used to go out for a walk through the moors and the hills, accompanied by his horse, Melmoth, that he rarely rode - he kept the animal by the reins, sometimes patting him and went on walking by his side, bending his head thoughtfully. He had his early morning walk every day, no matter if it was rainy or foggy.

"I need to have Melmoth on my side," he said, *"I need to feel the warmth of his breath snorting out from his nostrils, to stroke his massive muscles, to exchange glances with his wide bloodshot eyes - this creature of the earth helps me to keep the bond with reality and life."*

Once back, Melmoth's company was substituted by Ishtar, a tall specimen of a female Irish Wolfhound that he had adopted from one of his peasants and that used to trot constantly by his side, even indoors. He then used to take a light lunch and retire to his huge library. This room was one of his few delights, a large hall crossed by tall shelves filled with volumes of all sizes. His only passion remaining from his past was buying dozens and dozens of books, bought by Cezary in the main town's bookshop (he'd never have mingled with the people of the town). He passed many hours reading, at least *trying* to read.

"*I try to forget my own story, immersing myself in someone else's story.*"

But most of the time he was drawn into his own thoughts and the book hung from his hand, his other hand supporting his thoughtful forehead. Sometimes he went out again, keeping his mind busy with gardening, passing his time especially in his big glasshouse. He took care of the plants directly and, although in the gardens he enjoyed the aid of Cezary, he didn't allow anybody inside the glasshouse, except Ishtar. He often ended his afternoons with his forehead in a sweat, his sleeves rolled up, his arms covered with soil. Evidently his sense of life, having completely abandoned him, was still projected on the nature outside and perhaps this mere factor was enough to save his soul at that time.

He used to take another light meal, just the necessary to keep his energies up and, after dinner, always at the same time, he retired to the dressing room set in the west wing, sitting down in a chair in front of a blazing hearth, the faithful Ishtar crouching by his feet. Not a soul but Cezary and myself were allowed to enter the dressing room, not even the other servants. Cezary was charged to clean, to tidy up and all that was requested of him. Every evening, at the same precise time, *she* was there, sitting in the armchair in front of Lord K. They were sitting in silence in front of the grand fireplace, looking at each other.

"*I realized that all the strain – the long journey, the house hunting, the house restoring, the moving – all had been done in order to enjoy a moment like this.*"

She wore one of her dark, plain frocks that she used to

wear before being married to him. *"You dress like a nun, or a governess at best,"* he used to tell her when she was alive. He uttered those words in gentle mockery, smiling to her, to "his governess". Nevertheless, after marriage, she added some hints of colour to her everyday dress and maybe a ribbon to her hair now and then. However, these little arrangements could add nothing substantial - her image was fundamentally stuck to her original style and so was his remembrance of her too. After all, she remained "his own governess". Anyway, she used to keep him company, sitting down there, with some sort of white cotton cloth in her left arm, in which you would have surmised there was an infant. There was a child, indeed, *their* child. But not a sound, not a cry was to be heard from the bundle. Their child never saw the light. Their child was born just to die. And now he was bound to his mother's arm for eternity. There they were, back as a family. All gathered before the fire, like any other family throughout the country during evening time.'

A dense, glacial silence was growing in the little post office. Everyone was gaping - in each one of their eyes you could see, like many little mirrors, the ghostly vision of a bizarre domestic life.

'He was so pale and gaunt,' went on MacAllister, 'that I guess one wouldn't have recognised which one of the two was the phantom.'

'Did you ever see her?' asked Mr Toulson.

'Not at first. At least not with my eyes.'

'Can you explain yourself?'

'I suppose, at this point of the story, Lord K was the only one to see her. But the few times he allowed me to go in this room, I could without any doubt smell a pervasive, pungent odour.'

'What was it like? Can you associate it with something in

particular?'

'Certainly, it was unmistakable.' He stopped for a moment, unsure whether to continue.

'Blood.'

'Blood?' echoed Peter 'Are you sure it wasn't a scent coming from the kitchen downstairs? Maybe the cook chopping some meat?'

'Quite impossible: first, the kitchen is located on the northern side of the house; second, Lord K didn't take meat in his meals.'

A few seconds of silence elapsed, during which each one looked around as if to meet the other ones' eyes.

'My friends, I know you are skeptical and maybe you are laughing inside about the story I'm telling you, but let me go on before judging. I tell you, I was skeptical too. But there was no evidence of anything in the room to justify a similar, intense odour. Once I was admitted to take a seat, but he asked me to spare the chair in front of him and to take another one. Then he started to explain, but…ehm…I'm not sure you want to hear this part of the story. It's rather dismal.' He turned in particular to Mrs Wood, the only lady of the company.

'Oh never mind,' she exclaimed and everyone nodded. They evidently were too eager to know the rest of the narrative to be held back by their sense of horror.

'Well,' he went on, lowering his eyes, 'he told me, in confidence, that the last sight of her had been in their own bedroom, immersed in a blood bath – her own blood and their child's – her eyes enlarged, her mouth gaping. The blood stream had dropped from the bed onto the floor, leaving a horrible puddle. The nurses as well, naturally, had blood-stained faces and clothes. (Everyone instinctively gave a glance at Mr Reede's blood-stained apron). 'He said that he could never forget the scent. It persecuted him, it followed him everywhere. Even during the journey, even among the people. Finally, even in his new house in England.'

'Did you smell it just in that room?'

'Pardon?' MacAllister asked with distant eyes, engrossed.

'The blood smell. Was it just in the dressing room?'

'Yes yes…at least at the time. That room was *her* room, it was full of her belongings. Her portrait - the only human portrait in the house - hung above the fireplace: a long, slim figure, dark dressed, her black hair gathered in a neat bun behind her neck. Everywhere there were clues of her - her books, her brushes on the dressing table in front of the mirror, mingled with the coloured ribbons she used to embellish her hair. Even a sort of mannequin stood in a corner, with one of her frocks on and a crimson shawl wrapping the shoulders. It was as if she was there. She was alive. She was just out at the moment, taking a walk in the moors and you were expecting to see her approaching the threshold sooner or later, crossing the room and sitting by the mirror to brush her hair, disturbed by the moors' wind. But you knew that the truth was another: no Lady Lavinia was walking in the moors and the suggestion of her presence was reserved for the objects you discerned in the room. And yet they were no more than objects, cold and impersonal and she had gone, forever. Anyway, if she still haunted a place, it was the dressing room, exclusively there. No other rooms, nor the hallways, nor the gardens outside. The only 'outsider' in the room was Lord K's diary. It stood on the desk with a pen beside - a weird, isolated presence that was evidently out of place in a woman's room, the dark hard cover contrasting with the cheerful ribbons on the dressing table.

Sometimes, before going to bed, he sat down at the desk and wrote a few lines in his diary. I had no idea what they were about, but it's not difficult to guess, knowing his state of mind. He said it made him feel better that his diary was there, his more intimate reflections and feelings in his wife's room, among her clothes and brushes and books - he was sure that when he was out she was reading it, that's why he kept it visible on the desk and didn't place it in a drawer. Well, in connection with that, something occurred one day I was there - we were talking and suddenly he interrupted, looking at the empty chair in front of him. His eyes lifted and followed something or someone I couldn't discern. Then he stopped his gaze by his diary and there I saw – I swear upon my mother's grave – I saw the pages turning, by themselves. I mean, the windows were all fastened, the door locked, nobody was in but he and I. And the pages were turning, as if being read by somebody else. *"I suppose she wants to give you a further proof against your incredulity,"* he said.

I can assure you I needed no other proof at all, after this last event.'

'Didn't you feel frightened?' Mrs Wood dared to ask.

'Frightened? Well, maybe at the very beginning. I was more surprised than frightened - his calm manner made me feel at ease. He behaved as though nothing exceptional was happening. And actually it wasn't, from his point of view - Lady Lavinia's apparitions and deeds were part of his present daily routine. And he intended to introduce her to me with the same attitude with which he'd have introduced me to a living person.

And this is the point - he meant to communicate this event to me and not to anyone else. Rather than frightened I felt privileged that he wanted to share this incredible experience with me.'

'What about his servant?' observed Peter. 'You said that, together with you, he was the only one allowed to go in.'

'Cezary,' a queer smile appeared on MacAllister's face, 'was a curious fellow. Nobody ever fully understood his real nature. Mostly because he didn't speak a word in English, even if you couldn't really say he didn't understand our language. Lord K spoke with him in Polish - few, rather quick biddings about his tasks in the house and in the gardens. He treated him with calm and patience, the same manner you use towards an ill old person or towards a child. I suppose Lord K got annoyed by the excessive, silent affection paid by his valet and, instead of making him notice it, he was limiting the conversations between them merely to the tasks that needed to be accomplished. Further, Cezary never got on well with the other servants, showing no will to learn even a few words related to his job. This self-imposed isolation would have inevitably increased his idolatry towards his master and his dependency on him.'

'What about you?' Peter asked again, 'I mean you and Cezary - did you ever get in touch with…'

'He never spoke to me, for the aforesaid reasons,' interrupted MacAllister, 'but I'm deeply convinced that he was extremely jealous, as his master bestowed on me the confidence he'd have wanted for himself. He used to stare at me, whenever he was sure our master didn't notice it.'

'Why do you speak using the past? Is he…'

'Yes, he is. I will tell you how it happened when it is the right moment.' He got a draught of tea and took some time, so as to think more clearly.

'Where were we? Oh, yes…well, one of those dreary days was broken by the arrival of a letter. Just the sight of the envelope, marked with a coat of arms and a Polish address on the front, gave me a bad feeling at once. Lord K had urgently called for me and with an alarmed face silently handed me the letter. Obviously, I couldn't understand a word, but the very signature at the bottom startled me, the pompous handwriting showing a self-confident and conceited temper: it was the signature of his father-in-law. He briefly translated the content to me and, while he was explaining the situation to me, his restless eyes wandered anywhere and everywhere in the house, finding no place to rest. His father-in-law had never recognized Lord K's marriage with his daughter as legal, as long as it was done without his consent. While Lavinia was alive, he merely tolerated the circumstances for his daughter's sake. But after her death he felt justified in saying that Lord K was a profiteer and that he had no right to wander all across Europe with his money and to use the income from his possessions. Men like him project their own way of thinking and behaving upon all other human beings, you know, and the idea wouldn't occur to him that a man oppressed by grief would choose to retire from the world, rather than enjoy it.

I read a line of terror on his face. It was not the fact itself of being deprived of money and possessions that worried him, it was the idea of being forced to plunge into society once again. It meant going back to his profession, getting back in touch with the world. In other words, it was the mere thought of going back to life – real life – when inwardly he felt already dead.

"What can I do, MacAllister? What can I do?" he cried desperately. "I was even on the point of getting off the Doctors' Board, if it were not for my master, Professor Von Aschen, who prevented me from doing so, asking if I was mad. "Of course I am!" I answered, but he didn't allow me to give up for good. And now I see he was right, I see the evident necessity of pursuing my career again, unwillingly, in order to survive. To survive…" he laughed bitterly, he gave me goose bumps – "It means examining patients, getting in touch with colleagues, talking to people…I don't want to meet anybody, MacAllister. I don't even want to survive."

"Well, well, give me one night to study your papers - contracts, possessions, clauses and so on. I won't pass your house threshold tomorrow without a solution."

I spent the entire night over his papers, but it was just hopeless. One extreme solution occurred. Actually, I thought about a specific solution at the very first moment, but I had always rejected it every time it had entered my mind, as it seemed a real insult to his tragic story. At the end of the night, no other convincing solutions appeared and so I sadly took into consideration the one I had rejected. The problem was how to present this plan to him. Morning came and I passed Lastsight Hill's threshold.

When I was announced he approached me with an anxious face. "Well then?" he asked. I was ready to lower my eyes and humbly reveal my proposal. But suddenly I decided to be bold and I stared at him assertively.

He was listening to me silently and I could see his face getting grimmer and paler, his lips tightened even more than usual. He turned to the window, leant a hand on the frame above his head, glancing through the glass but actually seeing nothing. When I had finished my exposition, his hand leaning on the frame was clenching in a fist. He started in a low pitch, almost hissing like a snake. "How dare you talking to me about marriage?"

"Milord, I…"

"How dare you talking to me about marriage?" he repeated with a higher tone of voice. I never felt so bad in my life as I did at that time.

"MacAllister, you know me and all the most private details of my story and you're coming to me offering, as your best proposal, that I should marry again? Are you insane?"

"Milord, it's just because I know your story precisely and your need to be alone and severed from society that I'm proposing to you the only solution to keep your father-in-law from destroying your peace. Believe me, I've been considering all the possibilities, but there's no other safer way. Let me explain."

He finally turned towards me, composed himself and slowly sat down on his chair. He was looking at me suspiciously but at least he was inclined to listen.

"The countryside is full of families with young daughters to marry," I commenced. "They all place great expectations on a good match, capable of bestowing a little more comfort on the whole family. That's how marriage as an institution works at least - honestly, it's rarely a matter of feelings, love and…"

"Go on."

"Well…ehm…a marriage is basically a contract, Milord. It'll be no long and difficult task at all finding whichever local lady is disposed to give her signature in return for an entitled income. And once the lady is found, it's all done."

He lowered his eyes, brushing his chin with his fingers - at last he was considering the idea.

"But once she places her signature, she would make claims about this house, she would interfere with my life. MacAllister. I don't want a tiresome young lady in my house, speaking loudly, inviting her friends for tea, plaguing me with nonsense."

"We'll do our best to find the right lady. The main priority is preserving your peace, which has been threatened by a whim of your father-in-law and if an extreme deed needs to be done to assure it, let's do it. Do you trust me? Do you still think I'm insane?"

He lifted his eyes and answered.

"No. I don't. I never believed you were insane. And I trust

you."

I was going to leave him but he called me back from the distance.

"How will we choose her?" he shouted. "I have no intention of visiting every family in the surrounding countryside."

"Give me another night," I answered and at last I went.

The morning after arrived and again I was fervently passing his threshold.

As I went in I took a look around, as though I was visiting the house for the very first time.

"Well, what's your plan?" Lord K asked me abruptly.

I couldn't help smiling.

"A ball."

"A ball?!" Lord K repeated with dismay. "I can hardly understand you, MacAllister - first the affair of the marriage and now the absurd idea of a ball, in this house!" He shook his head. "I'll never do that, never."

"You will."

"Come on, MacAllister, stop it."

"You're not obliged to take part in it, even though you can easily have a good view of the guests." I looked again at the hall.

"What an absurdity - I'm not taking part in a ball promoted by myself, in my own house."

I was staring at him with half a smile. Once again Lord K slowly sat down on his armchair. "What an eccentric fellow you are, Julius MacAllister - your conventional and polite appearance easily deceives an external eye, but not mine. That's why I wanted you working for me - I immediately divined your originality under your elegant, good mannered British exterior. Come on - amuse me with your original ideas.'"

CHAPTER THREE

THE BALL

Dusk had surprised everyone and had gradually cast long dark shadows on the narrow streets of the little village.

A sudden angry knock was heard by the door - it was Mrs Reede, the butcher's wife, astonished to behold them, her husband included, chatting quietly there during dinner time. So the little company of the post office unwillingly decided to meet again the following day, in order to go on with the story-telling. Yes, unwillingly, because everyone would have remained, maybe all night long, such was the curiosity Mr MacAllister had induced in them.

And so they all gathered again the following afternoon. Mrs Wood, excited as never before, even brought some biscuits. Finally she popped in and, approaching the coffee table with her uncertain step, displayed them on it with a large smile.

'Finally the day of the ball arrived,' MacAllister went on as though nothing had interrupted the narrative from the previous day. In the background there was the noise of the wrapping from which the old ferret-lady tried with difficulty to draw out her cookies. 'I will spare you the madness of the days preceding the date of the ball, in a house normally devoted to silence and tranquillity. It's enough telling you that at certain moments it seemed to have reverted to the old times of Lord Coventry - the servants were running to and fro, portions of pork and beef were on the kitchen's worktops, such as you had never seen before. Lastsight Hill was caught by an unknown frenzy, as though a sudden tornado was whirling within it. The organization of the event was totally in my hands, following my own plan and some guidelines given by Lady Deville, the real promoter of the charity ball that we were merely hosting. Most of the time Lord K was outside on the moors with Melmoth and when he returned, if the house was still busy and noisy, he would directly withdraw to his room – *her* room – in the west wing. Sometimes, climbing the big staircase, he glanced downstairs in an odd way, amazed and surprised, as if he was in error and had entered someone else's house.

Yes, someone old enough to have taken part in Lord Coventry's parties, and knowing nothing about the subsequent story of Lastsight Hill, would have said that nothing had changed. Indeed, nothing had changed, were it not not for a sombre atmosphere that persisted in haunting the house. You could have breathed it. You would have immediately noticed that all the efforts to give the house a cheerful appearance were vain and that the change was just something transient, something artificial. Once the tornado had abated, everything would return again to the usual, reassuring mourning silence.

That very day, shortly before the first guests arrived, I took a look around me, glanced at the brand new upholstery and curtains which had arrived from the town for the special occasion, at the furniture of the hall moved aside to make room for the dancers. I had the same feeling you have when you observe an old woman trying desperately to dress and to make herself up like a young lady - all her attempts can't completely hide the impact of time passing. The same was so for the mansion. Its master's melancholy was perceivable everywhere, like a subtle dust settling upon everything - on the furniture, on the stairs, floating in the air you breathed. You couldn't escape from it. Nevertheless, we had to go on with the acting.

If Lastsight Hill was caught by frenzy, no less - in proportion – had happened in Mary Ann's cottage. With the remainder of the best material they had in the attic they tried to make up two dignified dresses and a rather refined gown was made for Daphne, on whom Mary Ann was setting all her hopes. But no spare material had remained for Page's gown and her mother was on the point to selling some of their hens to buy a new one. The young lady refused defiantly, saying that if the hens were sold she wouldn't take part in the ball at all. Then she fetched one of Daphne's old light gowns, a dress that her sister used when she was about fourteen, cut the fabric and added it to a top of the same colour, adjusting it here and there. "Do you see?" she said, proudly exhibiting the result to her mother and sister – "And you meant to sell our hens!"

November 10th 1900, evening.
A coach was waiting outside the little wooden gate.
"Come on, girls, it's time to go. Where's Donovan? Oh, naughty child, always idling around whenever we have to

hurry!"

"Don't be anxious mother, surely they're not waiting for us," said Page, descending the unfinished stepping stone path. She opened the gate and just outside it, by the last step, Bachmeier stood with his cigar in his hand.

"You all look marvellous!" He welcomed the three ladies with a bow and took off his hat with a large movement of his arm, bringing it next to his heart.

"Is he coming with us?" Page whispered in her sister's ear.

"Don't be rude, Page, of course he's coming with us."

Daphne was stepping into the coach when Page grasped her arm and whispered again.

"That is very upsetting - he's not part of the family."

"Oh please, it's as though he is. Furthermore, he arranged the coach service, otherwise we would have to walk there, as we don't have a coach at all, as you know very well. Stop it now, he will hear us.

"I don't mind."

Obviously Bachmeier had heard all the conversation, but he seemed not to be touched by it - he was aware of Page's distaste towards him.

The ladies were all seated in the coach, then he joined them and lastly Donovan arrived, running.

"Oh finally! Now we can go." Mary Ann bade the driver to leave and they all departed.

During the short journey it was Daphne's turn to whisper in her sister's ear.

"Remember what he did for you."

It happened indeed that, in the course of the last fortnight, Bachmeier had been ambassador of another piece of news brought to the Ashbys' house, which was another reason to feel grateful towards him. They were supposed to be good news, just a few days after the ball announcement -

you know the saying "bad luck comes in threes"? - it's the same regarding good luck. Well, a rich family of the surrounding countryside, the Phillips, was in need of a governess for the youngest daughter, a whimsical ten years old girl named Constance. Their last governess had suddenly married a local farmer – an unexpected and suspicious marriage that obviously aroused the consternation and the gossiping of the whole neighbourhood – and they hadn't found a substitute yet.

The fact came to Bachmeier's ear and he didn't waste time in recommending to them the name of Page Ashby, knowing very well her successful school training, her passion for reading and writing and her nearly perfect knowledge of the German language. After all, who better than Bachmeier could say that?

Just a matter of a brief interview with the girl's parents and Page started her job the very next day.

The Phillips' mansion was just a few miles from the village and she could reach it by walking or riding their little pony Holly. The proximity gave her the chance to come back home every night.

What a relief to give her family the security of a constant income.

What a hateful task to carry out, teaching to a bored, selfish, spoilt little girl who was looking through the window most of the time she was being taught.

"I'm not here to teach to a wall."

"You're paid to do that."

"I'm paid to teach *you*. Your parents will test you at the end of the year - what will you say?"

"I will say it's your fault. Who do you think they will believe?"

Her new job required a big mental effort and she came back home exhausted every night. But beyond this, something cheered her up. Constance's elder brother, Eugene Phillips, was well known for being a "poet laureate". This singular coincidence had naturally stimulated Page's curiosity and despite not having yet met him, a halo of admiration and awe surrounded the mysterious figure of this man. The only consolation of her job was the hope of meeting him some day and maybe exchanging a few words. She had no doubts that an immediate harmony would arise between them, as she was naively persuaded that poets share a natural common understanding about life and the world.

One evening, after her lesson, she escaped from Constance's room and was descending the stairs when she noticed a group of people gathered in the drawing room underneath - two young ladies seated on the sofa (presumably Constance's elder sisters) and two young men smoking by the fireplace. At the sight of them she was tempted to go back upstairs, drawn by her shyness, pretending to have forgotten something in Constance's room.

But one of the ladies noticed her and, glancing at the newcomer, murmured something in her companion's ear. The other lady turned towards the figure on the stairs and so did the gentlemen. Everyone was gazing at her. That was exactly what Page intended to avoid, but it was too late now.

"Good evening, you must be Miss Ashby, Constance's new governess." It was one of the gentlemen talking, an elegant chap with a thin black moustache and short black hair. While he was attempting this formality, the two ladies behind him hardly controlled their chuckles.

"Yes, indeed," she answered, descending the last steps. She couldn't help bestowing a harsh glance on the ladies.

"Well, I hope you will settle in fine in our house - my young sister's temper in not one of the best. By the way, allow me to introduce myself and the others: my name is Eugene Phillips, they are Martha and Sybil, my elder sisters and he is Mr Walsh, Sybil's husband."

Formal introductions made, Page dared to ask timidly, "So you are the poet, Mr Phillips, if I may ask?"

"Pardon?" he asked, surprised. He wasn't expecting such an address by a governess and neither was the rest of the audience.

"I heard you are a well-known poet, a poet laureate," she proceeded more hesitantly. Another burst of muffled laughs was audible.

"Oh yes, that's correct. Are you fond of poetry, madam?"

"Yes, I am," she blushed and grew angry with herself for blushing. She just felt unease and she wished she'd never raised the subject. "I mean, who is not?" she murmured awkwardly.

Mr Walsh came closer and, unasked, said abruptly, "Ladies shouldn't fill their heads with literature, especially with poetry. It makes them frown and have melancholic thoughts."

Young Phillips turned towards him but didn't say a word. For his part, Mr Walsh stared silently at her with a defiant demeanour.

How to resist such a provocation? But she ought to keep control. She couldn't disappoint her family. She ought to bring the money home.

Silence was growing heavy and the two sisters had stopped chuckling. They sat motionless with their gaze fixed on Page. Nobody could have ever surmised with certainty what feeling was prevalent in their countenance, whether it was consternation at the unhappy remark of Mr Walsh, which had touched a vulnerable point inside them as yet untouched by interiorized social conventions, or rather excitement for the potential reaction of the poor governess - after all one of their subordinates - and her consequent unavoidable further humiliation.

None of that happened.

"It's time for me to go. It's getting dark and I'm expected to walk a few miles. It was nice to meet you all."

She left the company and as she went Martha Phillips said aloud, "You have an unexpected admirer, brother."

"Why did you say that?" Young Phillips asked Mr Walsh, with no irritation in his voice, but rather with curiosity.

"Well, these governesses sometimes have such a conceit. They are convinced that they are your equal just by dint of the fact that they have some more notions in their brain than the average peasant folk. Further, I immediately noticed a peculiar pride on her countenance, it's good to rein her in at once and to make her understand she's an employee just like all the other ones - he hinted to the servants who were removing the tea service from the table.

So Page Ashby was thinking about this episode, at the whispering her sister bestowed on her ear as they journeyed to Lastsight Hill.

In spite of the blessing of having a new job, she had a double affliction: humiliations paid by the Phillips that she silently had to bear and of which this episode had been just the first; and a further, irritating reason to be grateful towards Bachmeier.

In the meantime the first guests had arrived and Lady Deville was welcoming everyone with large smiles. She was in her fifties, a good-looking woman. her eyes were light green and among her blonde hair just a few white ones were discernible by her temples. Her shiny necklace, consisting of excessively large green stones – that she meant to match with the colour of her eyes – emphasized conspicuously, with a disturbing contrast, the wrinkles on her neck.

She was perfect in her role, shaking hands and bestowing on each guest the right words to say on such occasions. Her husband, a tall man with a prominent stomach, stood dutifully beside her, repeating exactly the same things that she did or said.

It had been decided that the little orchestra would be seated on the stairhead, in the central hall. On each side of the band a wooden banister ran - a quite thick, crimson velvet curtain hung upon it, interrupted at four or five points, each a few inches wide, in which a gauze curtain hung. From there my master and I could observe unseen the people talking and dancing underneath.

"Those are Sybil and Martha Phillips - the second is unmarried. She loves spending all her winters in London, an important detail to know and yet more interesting if she is disposed to keep her habit after a marriage - your house will be quiet as long as possible then. The lady on the left is Miss Deville, our main guest's daughter. She's very young and noisy, I'd discount her, as she's fond of social life exactly like her mother. And that is..."

But Lord K was not listening to me. His eyes were fixed on a couple talking on one side of the hall. They had caught his attention and his curiosity. The scene didn't fit the context such as you might expect to see at a ball - just smiling faces and fragments of light conversations. It wasn't the case. The man, an elegant young chap dressed in a black suit, seemed to be having some difficulty keeping the conversation - his eyes were restless and he turned his face around now and then. The woman, a young lady dressed in a bright gown, first appeared surprised, as she was apparently interrupted by him in the middle of her speech. Then her brow frowned, her mouth tightened and her eyes betrayed a feeling you couldn't determine whether it was reproach or even contempt. Suddenly the young man turned and caught a glance from Lady Deville, who was strutting slowly, alone, at the bottom of the hall. With a quick bow he took leave of the young lady and went towards the main exit that gave onto the porch and from there directly outside, to the gardens at the front.

The poor young lady, to whom the glance between her friend and Lady Deville hadn't passed unnoticed, stood still there for a while, as if dazed. Then she noticed that Lady Deville herself was going outside too. She followed her with her eyes, still standing in place, as though incapable of moving. She seemed puzzled and bewildered at the same time. Finally she moved, finding her way with difficulty among the people crowding the hall, and went out.

During the time she was approaching the exit, my master turned towards me, bidding me to go out in the hall and entertain the audience with the announcement we had agreed before. Then I saw him disappearing through the stairs leading to the roof.

I have to make it clear that the entrance of Lastsight Hill faced a terrace. From there a huge central flight of steps led to the gardens as did a flight on each side.

"*Good evening ladies and gentlemen,*" I started my speech – a very simple, almost ordinary speech – as I emerged from the curtains and went before the orchestra. My master had in the meantime reached the roof and walked along the medieval battlements of the west wing.

'I'd like to introduce myself: my name is Julius MacAllister, Lord K's attendant. I'm glad you're enjoying this event, promoted by our marvellous Lady Deville". Everybody's eyes were seeking her, but she wasn't present. Her husband bowed gently and awkwardly, as all attention, in the absence of the aforesaid

lady, was diverted to him.

"At the same time, I'm sad to report to you that Lord K was obliged to remain far from here by an urgent affair, but he did his best..."

The young lady was now outside by the terrace, but she couldn't see the couple there.

"...he did his best to ensure that the ball would be a success..."

A young boy kept her attention, pulling her sleeve and then pointing his finger to a certain area of the park. She put her hand over the boy's shoulder, nodded at him as if to thank him and went towards the direction indicated.

"...and actually I'm ready to guess that it really is a success."

A clamour and a storm of applause followed, while the young lady in white walked through the darkness of the garden trees.'

Here MacAllister took a long pause to relish another cup of tea while the others were indulging animatedly in details about the ball reported by friends and relatives.

'Page Ashby was wandering about the hall. She had just left her sister, who had received an invitation to dance by a gentleman. Rather afraid that a similar invitation should be offered to herself, she had moved towards the furthest end of the hall. Her mother was talking in a lively manner with Mrs and Mr Allan, the new clothes shop owners, to whom she was introduced by Bachmeier - the very idea of joining their company and meddling in a discussion about the textile industry was not appealing at all. So nothing better remained than merely wandering about the room - sooner or later she had to find something to do or someone to talk to. Out of the corner of her eye she sensed the presence of Young Phillips. She wasn't sure that starting a conversation with him would be a good idea, but what else was there to do? At least they would talk about literature.

"Here she is," Martha Phillips murmured behind her fan with a smile. Her brother turned and the two sisters looked to each other - no, it hadn't been a good idea at all. But, again, it was too late.

"I didn't know you were invited," he said. Not a good start. "I mean, what a surprise."

"Well, it's surprising first to myself that I am taking part in this marvellous event." Immediately she despised herself for saying so.

"Did you take part in the events previously promoted by Lady Deville?" he went on. What a smart question - its aim was quite transparent. Of course she didn't. Nobody ever thought to invite her family to a ball. At least the music was loud enough to prevent his sisters from overhearing her answer.

"No, it's the first time." She lowered her eyes. Then she took courage to ask him the only questions he was worthy of being asked.

"Mr Phillips?"

"Yes?" he said distractedly. His eyes didn't focus on her face.

"As you are a poet, I'm eager to know what is a proper definition of poetry from your personal point of view? I'm always asking myself what..."

"Oh I see," he interrupted. He turned his face away and then, back to Page, answered hastily. "This delicate matter deserves a less noisy place to be discussed, don't you think? Further, I...I forgot to greet my old friend who has just arrived from London, I have to reach him. But I promise upon my word I will give you a detailed answer sooner or later." He bowed and went.

Page remained in her place, astonished by such an attitude. Again she regretted having approached him with the subject of poetry. His sisters were observing her through their fans. Such a fool she had been.

But something had happened beyond all that - while they were talking, Lady Deville was walking alone among the people, with a majestic pace, looking around her and smiling at everyone, as would be expected of her role. Suddenly she had smiled and stared at Young Phillips. Perhaps anyone else wouldn't have noticed, but Page caught in her demeanour a shade that was absent in the smiles and glances Lady Deville had bestowed on all the other guests.

He had reached the exit. He was going to welcome his old friend, as he had said, and apparently was going to meet him in the garden - a good smoking break among men in the open air.

Curiously enough, Lady Deville was also going outside. From where she was standing, Page could perceive her fine hairstyle, the thick green stones of her necklace shining in the chandelier's light. Page eyed her narrowly across the room and finally moved from the place in which young Phillips had left her. By now the frenzy of the dancers was rising and all the people, if not dancing, were crowding the sides of the hall, so it was very hard for her to make room for herself and to reach the exit.

When she got out on the terrace, nobody was there but two old men smoking.

"Page!" Somebody pulled her sleeve from behind.

"Donovan, what are you doing out here?"

"He's over there." He pointed towards an area of the park on the West side, behind the trees.

"Who do you mean?" she asked, pretending to be surprised.

"The poet," he answered shrugging his shoulders, as if his was the most obvious of answers.

She stood in silence, looking westwards. What was she

going to do? Much better it would be to go back to her mother and sister, pretending to enjoy "the marvellous event", as she had called it. But a sick, absurd curiosity was guiding her and suddenly she put her hand on Donovan's shoulder – "Thank you," she said. She walked down the side steps and disappeared.

Candles and torches had been set along the path that joined the big gate to the huge steps of the main entrance, so that the rest of the garden was plunged into complete darkness, except for the beams of a pale moon that revealed itself now and then from under ever-moving black clouds.

The big glasshouse stood right in the middle of the west lawns, reflecting on its panels sparkles of light coming from the manor house. A thick clump of bamboo trees separated the glasshouse from an arbour; this was surrounded by uncanny animal-shaped statues and finally by wild hedges, maybe at one time very neat and geometrically shaped. The arbour had a metal frame, on which creeping ivy was supposed to climb everywhere, but just a few yellow leaves dangled, devoured by a blight that nobody had caught in time. Lord K intended to get rid of everything and plant something else the next spring. But for now the trembling leaves hung neglected on the frame. The untrimmed hedges, which seemed like long-haired ogres, and the statues, which time and weather had modelled, added to the spot a further impression of forsakenness and it was not surprising at all that the decision had been taken to deprive this area of the gardens of light.

Four white marble benches stood by the arbour, one at each cardinal point. Behind the northern one a bush of red roses grew majestically, stealing from the visitor's eyes the attention once paid to the pervasive creeping plant.

The dark, supernatural stillness of the gardens, so at variance with the excitement of the dances inside the house, was unexpectedly crossed by a white spot. It walked alongside the glasshouse, whose plants remained indoors - *"they say he buried his wife's corpse in his glasshouse"* – and slowly went through the clump of bamboos.

"There she comes," a snake-like whisper was heard by the medieval battlements. The same person who had whispered, walking silently along the roof of the west wing, had previously noticed two other figures approaching the arbour, his attention caught by a sparkle of green stones standing out on a white-skinned neck. He had foreseen that somehow a collision would happen between them and the lady in white.

Page Ashby finally emerged from the trees and went forward, but she stopped behind a tall shaggy hedge, having seen the two figures moving under the arbour. She removed some twigs and watched: Lady Deville was lying back on the northern bench; she had bent her head backwards, in order to better offer her neck. Young Phillips was eagerly kissing her, sometimes taking the green stones in his mouth and sinking his face in her breast. The promoter of charity balls was laughing coarsely. The wrinkles on her neck seemed even deeper and more visible, in the heat of laughs and lust. The rose bush bent so imposingly above them, that it seemed as though sooner or later it was going to wrap the lovers up, in an inexorable grasp of thorns and blood red petals.

Page moved the twigs back in place and returned towards the house.

"Welcome to life," once again whispered the one on the battlements with unfeeling sarcasm. "You've received a very sad initiation indeed, poor little thing." He curled his lips curiously, gazing at the white, now tottering figure on her way back through the darkness.

He had uttered these last words with almost a devilish countenance: the satisfaction of a wretched soul witnessing someone else beaten and somehow humiliated by human misery.

He had been following the entire episode, from inside the house to the garden, with a sort of unwholesome curiosity. The poor lady was merely a stranger to him. Fostering cruel feelings towards strangers is easy. He felt the pleasing cold shiver of gratuitous cruelty running down his spine. It had made him forget his own personal misery for a while.

But then, gazing at the figure walking uncertainly through the trees of his gardens, something moved in his very soul and his devilish smile faded - the sweet bitter poison of his perversity had sunk inwards and, melding with his most genuine feelings, as in an alchemical transmutation, had turned into compassion.

She reached the glasshouse once again - a little wooden bench lay outside of it and she sat down, needing to remain alone a little more, her eyes still full of the scene she had just witnessed. Yet she was asking herself why she cared so much about it.

Not that Page Ashby was totally naive and out of touch with the darkest sides of life. At the age of eleven her beloved father died and with him all the happiness and comforts she had enjoyed. It was not really luxury that the Ashbys had known, but they had never suffered the lack of anything, her requests for a new doll or a new book had been never denied without serious educational reasons and her mother was never in the position of making clothes for her out of Daphne's old ones.

Suddenly all this lightness had been whirlpooled into her father's grave with him. But the sun hadn't always been shining when poor Joseph had been alive either. She remembered bitterly that, on some evenings, a sort of bad spell was cast across her mother's face. It happened when her father was out and didn't come back home in time for dinner.

"Where is daddy?"

Mary Ann produced a different answer every time, reaping the best of her imagination, inventing plausible accidents that could have happened to him. But Page had never believed her, nor Daphne - as children often do, they remained in their role, nodding and showing they really believed what their mother told them. But, as soon as they heard daddy's uncertain steps on the path and his rough altered voice, they glanced at the bewildered face of Mary Ann and, without waiting for any order from her, they knew perfectly well what to do, hurrying silently at once to their room.

Her beloved, weak father. She hated him for that, with the same intensity, in proportion, as that with which she had loved him.

With time Daphne seemed to have forgotten – or removed – this part of their life; at least she had never mentioned it to her sister. By contrast, it had stamped an indelible mark on Page.

But how did it occur that these events had crossed her mind right now?

She glanced at the plants in the glasshouse - they seemed to be disturbed by the music and the clamour coming from the house, although muffled because of the distance.

"They say he buried his..."

She didn't pay attention to her silly little brother's words. She felt as if she belonged more to the silent azalea, to the wild cactus and to the cheerful lemon trees immersed in the peaceful darkness of the park, protected by the glass panels – than to the humanity inside, and she lazily leant her head on the glass, as if to be in touch with them in some way.

Her senses were dazed, her mind confused. So when she caught, out of the corner of her eye, a dark figure wandering among the battlements, she ascribed the event to her harrowed imagination. The same with regard to what seemed to be a woman's profile, at an unlit window right underneath the battlements, which was visible in the dark because of an extraordinary, nearly cadaverous pallor that made the woman's face appear outlined against the dark backdrop. Page turned her head away, incredulous, but suddenly turned it back again, as if prompted by a misgiving - the two figures had both disappeared. Yes, surely it had to be her imagination. If not, they had to be nothing more than servants. The one on the roof was probably taking his turn at watching the mansion from above – these balls are always a good occasion for robbers who take advantage of the general confusion – and the woman at the window was undoubtedly a servant who was alarmed with suspicion on seeing someone walking in the unlit gardens. Yes, it was as she had thought. Who other than a servant, during a cheerful event like that, would withdraw into the solitude of a dark unlit room, while everyone was supposed to enjoy the party? *"Perhaps nobody but someone like me,"* she thought as she sat there alone in the dark, with the sole company of the plants of the glasshouse.

She needed to go, before a member of the household, suspecting her to be an intruder, went in vain to alert me or, worse, Lady Deville. *"Oh no, please, let's avoid this further embarrassment."*

She got up and took her way. She was still unsteady but in her mind she was resolute that she would leave the party as soon as possible.

It was not just having seen Young Phillips involved in such a situation - it was something more subtle and more powerfully disturbing at the same time.

It was like having pushed another, secret door. One of those doors whose existence was pretty much known, but which was concealed by silence and lowered eyes.

Behind one of those doors stood her father, in the state he was in on the nights when he didn't come back in time for dinner: drunk, altered, violent.

Behind the door she had just now pushed stood the scene she had beheld a few minutes earlier.

She realized furthermore how she despised Young Phillips, the poet whose sensibility she had been so certain of previously - she had genuinely admired his culture and his fame as a poet, even before having met him. But, once she had met the man, his pride and vanity had set him very low in her esteem. Until now, young Phillips had never bestowed any real attention on Page Ashby - she was his sister's governess and one of his admirers, that was enough. His embarrassment at his sisters' giggles or at his brother-in-law's rudeness was due just to politeness and formality - nothing excluded the likelihood that his opinions conformed with theirs. His exchanges with Miss Ashby were limited to occasional brief meetings at the end of her classes and he was accustomed to accept her humble compliments with smugness, bestowing here and there some polite comments and smiles.

She had been keeping her eyes stuck to the ground for the whole duration of her walk, but now that she was in the proximity of the house, at the foot of the steps, she lifted her thoughtful eyes and stared at the mansion. She was observing all the heads and shoulders whirling at the music, beyond the huge mullioned windows of the hall - ladies with smiling faces and superb hairstyles, gentlemen with proud demeanours and neatly combed hair.

The massive chandelier cast upon all of them a shining, cheerful light that revealed with no doubts what they actually were - joyful, hopeful, blooming youth.

The bright light on the inside played a strange, sinister contrast with the gaunt profile of the mansion seen from the outside. Its dark, heavy shape stood on the cloudy, ever-changing skyline like an old lady dressed in mourning, knelt down on a graveyard, resolved to stay before her beloved's gravestone and never to leave it.

Suddenly she felt that the light of the chandelier, so cheerful and shining, had something tragically ironic about it, regarding the whirling youth underneath, and partially herself too: they were all young, yes, and hopeful and fresh, true. But they were vulnerable as well - young flesh ready to be shot by the unpredictable arrows of life and destiny.

Finally she climbed the steps and reached her mother. Mary Ann almost ran towards her daughter as soon as she perceived her, approaching with a desperate face.

"Guess what? Lord K is not here! He was held up somewhere by an urgent affair, can you believe it? Oh I knew that I would have to resign myself forever to my endless bad luck! But look at you, my dear, you look terrible, what happened to you?"

"I'm feeling sick, I think I'm going to ask Bachmeier to use his carriage to go home."

"Don't think to leave alone, Page."

"I must leave alone, mother - how can you abandon all your hopes at once? Look, it's full of young gentlemen, let Daphne enjoy the dances," she hinted at her smiling sister, involved in a fast dance in the middle of the room, "and I can go by myself, I don't need anyone to come along with me."

"Well, maybe you're right. But stay here, I will ask Mr Bachmeier for you."

So she turned to reach him, leaving Page temporarily alone.

"Miss Ashby," a voice tragically familiar came from behind her.

"No, please, not now."

She didn't turn, pretending not to have heard.

"Miss Ashby," this time the voice was louder - impossible to go on pretending. The face of Young Phillips appeared suddenly from behind her shoulder. She shrank instinctively. She didn't mean to, but couldn't help it, and he noticed it.

"I just thought about the question you asked me. Maybe now..."

"Very kind of you, but I'm going." She had spotted Bachmeier. He winked at her - he walked on, passing by her and saying aloud "The coach is ready, Fräulein".

"Already going?" asked Young Phillips surprised.

"I'm not well," she said walking backwards, but without looking at him and with a certain air of disdain.

"But you have much worthier reasons to enjoy yourself tonight, Mr Phillips. See you another time, good night."

She went through the exit, Bachmeier waiting for her at the top of the steps. His half smile and sparkling eyes betrayed that he had clearly understood that he had saved her from an awkward situation. She grew irritated, once more, but didn't hesitate to rush down the steps and make haste towards the coach waiting in the distance.

Young Phillips had followed her white figure, seriously looking at her for the very first time. He was accustomed to deem Page Ashby as a cleverer than average girl who worked as governess in his house, nothing more. But now he hadn't seen such a young lady, he had seen a woman. She had a new shadow in her eyes. Even her skin seemed to be different and her freckles were no longer a matter of funny jokes about a teenage Irish face - they were a gentle, refined decoration on a noble, beautiful ivory skin. And never mind the slightly purple shadows under her eyes, the result of the drudgery at her own house and gardens or of her struggles with his whimsical sister - they now underlined so marvellously her premature maturity. He was so convinced she liked him – just as he was convinced that he was admired by everyone – that her leaving, notwithstanding her healthy reasons, disappointed him a little. But mostly he was sorry.

Why hadn't he noticed her before? He stood observing her light figure in the distance, getting in the coach and disappearing.

Both Page Ashby and Eugene Phillips were unaware that they were observed by a third one on the roof. He had witnessed the change in her attitude, the subsequent sordid episode by the arbour, as well as Phillips' change in his consideration towards the young governess.

And all of them were unaware that a fourth element – an unearthly element - was observing them all, tracing their inward feelings and tragically foreseeing their own destinies.'

CHAPTER FOUR

BACK TO REAL LIFE WITH SURPRISES

'Page had left at the ball a desperate mother and a disappointed sister, even though the latter had soon recovered by enjoying the dances. Therefore she was naturally surprised to be woken up in the middle of the night by an excessively excited Mary Ann.

"Page, Page, guess what?" She turned her face to the other side. She had had very odd dreams during her short rest and she wasn't disposed to listen to silly reports from a ball. "It was a lie, Lord K never left Lastsight Hill!"

"What?" she opened one of her eyes.

"Yes, Mr Bachmeier revealed it just on our way back," her sister clarified while sitting on the side of the bed. "He feared that, had he revealed it earlier, we would have been tempted to spoil the secret. He said it was all done on purpose - in reality Lord K was observing everyone from above."

"Why did he do that?" asked Page drowsily.

"Oh I don't know. I suppose it's because of his misanthropy."

"Never mind," interrupted Mary Ann, "that means that we still have hopes and I think our Daphne will have no competitors in that - she was so pretty, she was admired by everyone, wasn't she? Did you have a look at the Phillips or the Wellnocks? They seemed all consumed by envy to perceive how many times Daphne had received an invitation to dance!"

"Don't exaggerate, mother. Elsa Deville also received a lot of invitations."

"Oh, don't consider her at all - she's Lady Olivia Deville's daughter. Of course all the gentlemen invited her because they want to gain favour with her prestigious family! And surely that lady won't need to struggle to find a husband."

"The market reopened, then," Page whispered half asleep.

Daphne's face darkened.

"Well, I'm really tired, I'm going to sleep," she said. "Good night, dear Page, we're leaving you alone now."

"Good night."

Daphne left the room, but Mary Ann was lingering there and Page sensed her presence.

"Mother?"

"Yes, child, tell me."

"Are you feeling comfortable with the prospect of giving Daphne to a man you have never met and who was so strange as not to mingle with people during a party in his own house?" she said slowly. "And what about all the oddities they say about him?"

In one of her nightmares she had dreamt about the huge glasshouse at Lastsight Hill - among the lovely lemon trees and the white azaleas a large pit was in the ground. From a distance it looked as though it had been dug on purpose to give room for a huge plant, but on approaching it, it was clear enough that there wasn't a plant inside the hole - there was a human corpse. She didn't want to tell her mother about it.

Mary Ann remained silent for a while.

"Page," she whispered, "what do you think about marriages? Maidens go to the altar having met their future husbands very few times before that moment."

That was unexpected.

"But you knew our father very well, didn't you?" she managed to say. "You were in love, weren't you?"

"Yes, child, we were. That's why we had the world against us and we were all driven mad."

"Not you, mother."

"What?"

"You're not mad, you're brave."

"Good night, my dear." She stroked her daughter's red hair and went out.

"Good night."

The following days continued with the usual regularity of tasks. But something different was in the air, a sort of suspense that gave to their ordinary life a sweeter taste. Daphne was smiling
silently all the time, as though she was keeping an exciting secret. Mary Ann had a peculiar gaiety in her manner, even in reproaching Donovan or trying to catch the hens. Gertrude herself, usually so severe and strict, looked more relaxed, as a result of the light atmosphere in the house and one could frequently catch her singing some folk tunes in German while sweeping the floor or picking up vegetables. Regarding Page, she had a radical change in her everyday life, something maybe regarded as not important by the

others, but extraordinary for herself. After she had begun working with the Phillips the attitude of the other members of her family towards her had gradually changed, as if, for the mere fact of her bringing home an income, she had suddenly passed directly from the childhood to the adult phase. Mary Ann and Daphne even encouraged her to retire in the library, instead of detaining her to help with the housework. "You have to prepare your next lessons," they said in a low voice, gently shutting the library's door. And whenever Donovan spoke too loud, they promptly hushed him – "Your sister is studying!" She could hear their comments and scoldings from inside the library and they made her smile.

This was definitely a radical change for Page.

Her strong passion for literature had always been considered a "reverie" or a "silly hobby", something that could lead to nothing helpful for them.

But now the connection of her "silly hobby" with money had created a halo of reverence around her person and her mother in particular treated her, when she came back from the Phillips, as she would treat a very special guest. All this naturally pleased her, but her inner intuition, so sharp for a young lady like her, could sense a lack of authenticity in it that made her feel uncomfortable - money had suddenly elevated her, overnight, to dignified, well-deserving adult status. Why did people behave like that? Why couldn't persons and things simply be considered for what they were and not for the income they could bring with them?

As a matter of fact, regarding her external appearance, no one could call her "a girl" anymore. She had had to modify her ordinary attire and style, firstly subduing her habit of keeping her hair wildly loose and yielding to having a neat, decent hairstyle, appropriate to her job; secondly, she was forced by her new role of governess to wear dark frocks, tightened at her neck by a high collar. Dressed up in this style, with her professional bag, her books in her hands and a black bonnet on the top of her head, she looked like an adult woman to all intents. Young Phillips had furthermore noticed that and was waiting for her to descend the stairs every evening at the same time, knowing perfectly when she had finished her tuition. But she always went away in a rush, eluding his requests for her to stop for a cup of tea. Luckily she had plausible reasons to adduce - helping mother with the dinner, finishing some sewing work, and similar. But he was not exactly the kind of stupid man she thought he was - he knew human nature enough to understand that she was avoiding him. Eventually his vanity suggested to him that her continuous rejecting of him wouldn't last too long and the pressure of their being daily in contact under the same roof would lead to surrender, sooner or later. It was just a matter of patience. So he thought.

The only one thinking that under the new garments there was the same soul as before, was Page herself. Nothing had decreased her freedom of thought and her deep link with Nature, which she was forced to entertain just during her walks to the Phillips' house and back. During her journeys she would free her mind to go wherever it wanted to roam. But no more excursions to the moors for the moment and she missed them terribly. In exchange she was having much more time for herself and her books every evening - no intruders, no noise, no feeling guilty for being there in the library instead of helping mother. She had begun to deem the hours of tuition with the moody and spoiled Constance as an unavoidable fee to pay, a sacrifice she ought to commit, in order to deserve her moments of peace and solitude. Young Phillips' attempts to hold her were just a further hindrance to the accomplishment of her daily goal.

It's true that a mutation was taking place within her, working inwardly since the night of the ball. But it had been just the beginning, like the prow of a vessel breaking the ice at the North Pole and the vessel now keeping its way smoothly through the icy land. She had taken on a different, a disenchanted view of people and life.

What was worrying her presently was the childish manner of her mother and sister, trapped in a sort of perpetual illusion and dreaming vainly about positive implications for their future life.

She sometimes lifted her eyes from the books up to the window - she used to keep the curtains drawn apart, as if she wanted to keep a connection with the world outside. The window faced the back yards and the countryside beyond. Over that hill, out of her sight, her father's grave was lying, on the slope on which the churchyard spread. Further beyond, on the right, the dry white road led to Lastsight Hill. She was sincerely worried about her dear sister and she really hoped, deep in her heart, that the illusion would soon be dispelled, that Lord K would marry a rich bored lady and would leave Daphne alone, back to reality. No illusions of a wealthy life anymore. No more legends about wives' corpses in the greenhouse, no more stories about never-ending mournings and black suits.

Two more weeks passed and still no news had circulated about this affair. Bachmeier had rarely popped into their house and when he did, he talked merely about general matters. With a sense of relief she had noticed that the triumph had faded from her mother's face and from Daphne's as well - they were starting to realize that the dream had to finish and the skill with which Bachmeier avoided the subject underlined her conviction.

But on a mild evening of November, she had to change her

mind.

She had had a very difficult day with Constance. The girl was on the verge of insulting her and she was on the verge of shouting at the girl. The only good thing she could do was to have a break for a while. She had left Constance reading alone in the room and had passed fifteen minutes in the family library, waiting for her nerves to calm. Luckily no members of the family were wandering about, Mrs Phillips being always in town during daytime and Young Phillips in the garden with some friends. The mild weather of the day, really extraordinary for late November, had encouraged them to have tea outdoors and she could observe his figure from the library window, telling some of his jokes to the ladies and smoking his cigar. Everyone seemed to hang on his lips.

What a distorted idea of poetry they all had.

She had finally read some lines of his - very rhetorical, but in their own style smart poems, that would have undoubtedly pleased any representative of his rank. How he had obtained the title of "poet laureate" she never understood.

Well, that hard day of tuition had finished at last and she was about to go on her way back home. She was walking along the drive leading to the gate. Her eyes' shadows were even more purple than usual and her cheeks were a little bit hollow. Young Phillips perceived her from the distance and he parted from the rest of the company. His sisters noticed that something new was in the air.

"Miss Ashby!" He rushed towards her waving his white hat.

"*That's all I needed,*" she thought. She was so exhausted, she just wanted to go home and this time she wouldn't have even opened a book.

"Miss Ashby, why don't you join us?" He realized how the signs of tiredness enhanced the beauty on her face. Later on he would write a poem about it, *To a Weary Beauty*.

She looked at him surprised. "*Join you? To listen to your nonsense?*" she went on thinking.

"Very kind of you, Mr Phillips, but I'm really tired and..."

"You always run away," he said and she noticed a little embarrassment in him. She had never seriously considered, all this time, a changing of interest on his part towards herself.

He turned his head towards the company. "We're having some tea on the grass, maybe it can be relaxing for you. I know what you are going through with Constance, we already changed at least three governesses."

"Indeed? I thought there was just one before me."

He hesitated and then asked again.

"So...what about my invitation?"

What was she going to do now? She didn't want to join the party at all, but she had always refused any previous invitation. Which formula was the best to appear polite without disappointing his expectations?

"Well, thank you, but just for a while." She cursed her excessive politeness.

It was the worst afternoon of her life.

Both her attire and her attitude unavoidably highlighted her difference from the other ladies. The presence of Phillips' brother-in-law, Mr Walsh, had upset her even further. She had never forgotten what he had said on that evening about women and literature. The level of conversation was really very poor, inducing her to participate just with laconic comments. Young Phillips appeared more excited and nervous than usual, excessively talkative sometimes. He was insisting on the matter of poetry, pressing her to tell them something about her favourite authors. She felt uneasy but it was a kind of uneasiness different from the first time, when she was observed by them while descending the stairs and a blush had coloured her cheeks. This time irritation was the prevalent feeling inside her. She considered poetry as something holy, something to handle with care, something to whisper about, not exactly an object of idle chats. They were exhibiting their indeed scarce knowledge with a ridiculous pride and vanity, talking aloud, using poetry as entertainment or as an object to boast about, like a new bonnet or a golden watch. They were bent on drawing her into their flow, but she just wanted to escape from them.

The difference between her and the ladies around had impressed Young Phillips to the point of feeling proud of having discovered such a treasure - in his own way he was a man of letters and he could recognized a higher spirit when it was in front of him. He had perceived her cultural superiority notwithstanding her very young age and nothing more needed to be added to his already existent infatuation. During her journey home Page felt her head aching. She really would have preferred to have worked a whole day in the fields rather than pass a day like that again. She untied her bonnet and let her hair down, in a liberating gesture. She felt the chill wind of November on her face, closed her eyes and took some deep breaths. Oh, what a relief! All alone, just the wind of the moors as company...

Then she made haste forwards, as dusk had already set.

But her day wasn't finished yet. As she crossed the gate her mother appeared on the threshold with a dismal face.

"Where have you been? And what about your hair?"

"I was held up by..."

"There's no time; Lord K will be here in a while."

"Lord K?"

"Mr Bachmeier came in the morning, informing me that Lord K asked to call this evening. Everything is ready, Daphne is marvellously dressed! But we expected you home at the usual time, dear - why did you delay, today of all days? Go, go upstairs, comb your hair and change your shoes, they're completely muddy! Oh no, there's no time, stay here." She stopped, alarmed. "Mr Bachmeier is arriving with him!" She bade Gertrude to open the door.

Page found her mother's excitement a little ridiculous and sincerely hoped she would keep control during the interview.

Gertrude opened the door but Bachmeier alone entered.

He greeted them as usual and bestowed a curious glance on Page. She didn't like his half smile. He surely had known long ago about Lord K's wish to meet Mary Ann, why had he kept silent?

"Lord K's coach is on the way," he commenced. "He will be here in few minutes."

"Page, sit down there. Gertrude, you fetched the tea service I told you to, didn't you?"

"Yes, Madam."

Page sat down and at once perceived the top of a dark coach stopping in front of the house.

"And do not serve the biscuits until I bid you to."

A valet was opening the wooden gate.

"Gertrude, call Donovan out of his room, please!"

A tall, dark-suited man crossed the garden on the unfinished stepping stone path.

"Finally, we're all here. Daphne will enter later. Sit down there, Donovan."

Lastly Gertrude opened the door.

The same tall man that had crossed their front garden entered the house. From the very moment Page had seen him outside - so thin and tall with his high black top hat, his black hair springing from it and his walking stick - it had seemed to her that she beheld, as she said later on, "*a fictional character sprung from my imagination.*"

He could not be real. He wasn't entering their house. He had nothing to do with their life of common people.

He came in without saying a word, just taking off his hat and lightly bowing his head as a greeting. He had given up his daily clothing for the occasion, but not the mourning colour - he had chosen an elegant suit, a silken shirt and a large cravat, all of them totally black.

Naturally Mary Ann overwhelmed him with her talking and it was immediately visible that she was bothering him. Bachmeier's words about Lord K's misanthropy and his unsociable temper echoed in their minds.

"My daughter Page and my son Donovan. Please, have a seat over there. I will check that everything is ready for the tea."

In the few seconds in which Mary Ann was in the kitchen to give Gertrude further instructions, Page couldn't resist - she lifted her eyes, scrutinizing their weird guest. With much surprise she found that he was doing exactly the same with her, with no qualms at all. She was not used to such a frank, almost impudent attitude but, as though bewitched, she didn't lower her eyes. Bachmeier had described him right - he was really gaunt and incredibly pale, nearly frightening. He was much younger than she had thought but his sharp features lent him a grim look, making him appear older than he actually was. Gradually Page realized he was literally consumed by his grief and his eyes, far from being scary, were sad and nearly screaming out their melancholy.

She felt compassion. How curious. If only he had divined her feelings at that moment, the same that he had experienced in watching her from the battlements of his house, a fortnight earlier.

She felt she had to break the awkward silence.

"My sister will arrive soon."

How clumsy. For what reason had she mentioned her sister? Nobody had said he was there for that reason, at least not officially. Luckily her mother didn't overhear.

Lord K could hardly believe that the lady in front of him now was the same he had perceived in the distance the night of the ball - on that occasion she was dressed in white and had her hair gathered neatly behind her neck, conforming to the style of all the other ladies. Now he was beholding a governess in a black frock, with hair wildly loose on her shoulders - its lively red colour contrasting with the dark coarse material - her face marked by deep purple shadows under her eyes. His glance lowered unavoidably to her muddy old boots and with that the picture of her was complete: very confusing indeed. It seemed that rigour and freedom were coexisting in the same person and he couldn't formulate any clear opinion from these first appearances.

Mary Ann came back and sat down next to Page.

It was a very embarrassing situation, as he persevered in staying silent.

"So, Mr Bachmeier informed me that you would like to talk with me..." finally ventured Mary Ann.

"Do you live alone here?" he asked abruptly. His deep voice seemed to rumble in the room. Page and her mother looked to each other. He surely wasn't accustomed to formalities and conversations.

"Yes, my children and I live here, with our housekeeper Gertrude." Right at that moment the tea was served.

"She is from Hamburg, near to your city, isn't it?" Gertrude shook her head looking sternly towards Mary Ann.

"Don't you have any other servants?"

"Oh no, not for the moment. We used to have." Mary Ann felt uneasy under his inquisitive eyes and frank questions. "The truth is that my daughters are really good at doing all the housekeeping. Other servants would be superfluous." Page felt embarrassed and sorry for her mother.

Eventually Mary Ann thought that the best thing to do was to call for Daphne and so she whispered a few words in Gertrude's ear.

The housekeeper went away and after a while Daphne appeared on the top of the stairs.

Page looked at her delighted - her sister was marvellous in her new gown. Mary Ann had obtained it thanks to an agreement with the Allans, the clothes shop owners. They had agreed that Mary Ann should attend to the numerous little tasks of mending for their clients, in exchange for which she would give up the dress making, shifting all the selling to the Allans. As an incentive for their new agreement, the Allans had given her two gowns for her daughters.

"All this strain to please a sad man who doesn't care at all for formalities and well-tailored clothes," so Page thought while her sister was descending the stairs, noticing a complete indifference on Lord K's face.

On contemplating her daughter Mary Ann grew radiant and got up to welcome her. "She's Daphne, my elder daughter." He got up and bowed, as a gentleman. But then he sat down and went on talking with the same plain tone as before, as if nothing had happened.

"I was told you have a little plot just outside the village, haven't you?"

"Yes indeed," answered Mary Ann a little surprised. "We're harvesting it and selling the crops at the town market."

"Is it giving a good income?"

"Well, I dare say it's enough for our needs. My children and I are content with what we have."

"It is not their merit, you raised them so."

"Oh, so kind of you, but I have to say they were born with a very good temper, both of them, even if they are very different from each other."

"What about me, mother?" the voice of Donovan echoed in the room. She had nearly forgotten about his presence. She glanced at him with reproach, then smiling she said, "Oh, certainly, you too are good-tempered. By the way, maybe you will play something at the piano for our guest, won't you?"

"Oh please, spare me this."

An icy silence descended on them. The harsh, deep voice of Lord K had had a freezing impact with this last utterance.

Page exchanged a glance with Donovan - they would have burst into laughter if only they had been alone in another room. How could Mary Ann repair that, now? She was feeling almost desperate; she had never thought he was so nasty until this point. But suddenly he raised his voice.

"Mrs Ashby, I need to have a word with you alone."

This came really unexpectedly, as the preceding conversation hadn't been promising at all.

Without wasting further time, the girls and Donovan got up at once, while Bachmeier moved to the library.

Once out of the room, Page approached her sister, seriously concerned about Daphne's possible future under the same roof with such a strange man. But Daphne's face surprised her - clearly her sister seemed disturbed but somehow fascinated by the odd manners of the stranger. He was so extraneous to the life and the habits they normally led, that it was unavoidable not to be affected by him, in a positive or in a negative way, or in both. As a matter of fact the same impression had struck Page herself, but she was still too confused about their guest.

Daphne didn't let her speak - she hushed Page, putting a hand on her mouth, and went towards the sitting room door, leaning her ear to the panel in order to eavesdrop.

"Daphne, don't..."

"Shhh!" Daphne hushed her again and with a gesture of her hand invited her sister to do the same. At last Page approached and tried to peep. The door consisted of two panels, and once closed a narrow chink remained between them. Donovan joined them, crouching at the floor.

If someone could have beheld them from behind, the picture would have been rather funny: the red curly hair of Page on the top, right underneath Daphne's profile in the effort of listening, and finally the amused Donovan on the floor, in reality not listening at all, but just excited at being allowed to stay there with his elder sisters, outside of the rules of conduct, as he had always been taught not to peep or to eavesdrop at the doors.

After a while the amusement faded and disconcert appeared on the girls' faces, until Daphne, bewildered and silent, slowly left the door and went out to the front garden. Page remained by the door as if stunned, while Donovan was looking at her questioningly from below.

"Mrs Ashby, I won't take much of your time, I will be straightforward. I am not here to have a chat with you, I am here to ask for your daughter's hand."

Mary Ann, disappointed and confused by the interview hitherto, was naturally overwhelmed by joy on hearing such a proposal - all her efforts had not been in vain! She recovered and started to say, stammering a little, "I felt that it was all about this, I swear! Oh, dear Lord K, I'm so honoured and I'm sure you have made the right choice with..."

"I am obliged to be quite honest with you from the beginning, Madam. I lead a very lonely life, as you probably know and I am not quite sure my lifestyle would please a young lady."

"I know, I know. It won't surprise you that Mr Bachmeier informed me about it."

"Yes, that German gentleman seems to know many things."

Mary Ann coughed, embarrassed.

"But however you learned it," he went on, "it is true and I am really determined to carry on my own life exactly in the same way I led it hitherto. I bet that Mr Bachmeier told you the reasons for my need to re-marry. And, as far as I understand, my need matches your aspiration to a better life, despite your attempts to mask your anxieties, a circumstance that I perfectly understand. I will be frank - you will enjoy a wealthy income from this agreement."

"I am sure Daphne will guarantee you your peaceful life without bothering you at all."

He stared at her silently, pointing his fingers to his chin. "Mrs Ashby..."

"Yes?" she grew alarmed - what further odd conditions was he going to ask?

"I am afraid we are at a misunderstanding."

She stared at him, incapable of uttering a word. What was going on now?

"I'm not here to ask for Daphne's hand. I'm here for your younger daughter."

Outside the room a little drama was going on.

Daphne was in the garden, leaning on the fence. Page, after few minutes of astonishment during which she had been incapable of moving, slowly reached her sister. Daphne's face was obviously upset, tears were ready to shed but still hesitating in her eyes, in a mixture of disappointment, rage and delusion. In a sense Page was delighted by that. It meant that her sister was not entirely the monument of self-immolation to duty she had always known, always pleasing other people and willingly accomplishing all the tasks requested of her without any complaint. Daphne hid a little core of pride and the present event was a demonstration of that, even if to Page it remained a wonder how it could be a source of pride to be promised to a stranger.

"Daphne, I will never..."

"Wake up from your reveries, silly girl, you *must* marry that man!"

Page was stunned by such a reaction.

"Our financial situation is miserable and even if you carry on working as governess for years we'll never cover our debts. Lord K is right, you've heard what he said to mother - you are silent, you like solitude and you don't fancy balls and clothes like any other lady. You...you're different. You know that, sister." She had lowered her voice and her eyes. "You are the perfect lady for his purpose and I was wrong to be angry just now. I was just hurt in my vanity. Please forgive me," she held her sister's hands, "and do not worry about living with him. It's not a real marriage, after all. You'll be free, you'll have time for yourself, more than now, and we shall meet whenever we want to."

Page was looking at her as if in a bad dream. What was she talking about? Was she talking about herself? It couldn't be possible. The unreal character that had stepped into their house and messed up their life would vanish as silently as he had arrived and everything would go back to its ordinary routine.

Daphne hugged her and in doing so Page sensed that inside

the house Bachmeier was looking at them from behind the curtains. When their eyes met he sneered and turned away. She shivered with rage: he knew.

It had gone all too fast.

She was alone in her room now, lying on her bed on top of the blankets, still wearing her frock. The hard morning with Constance, the even harder afternoon on the grass with Young Phillips and now this. But the third event had something different from the other two. These were transitory - if she so wished, when overcome by exasperation, she could quit her job; if she so wished, when annoyed by his attention, she could decide not to bestow a single word on Young Phillips anymore. But *that*...that was forever. It was her future, her life. To link her own destiny to a sad, grumpy widower was the last event she had ever thought could occur in her life. Even in her oddest "reveries", as her sister had called them, she'd never have thought about a hypothesis like that. Actually, she had never thought of linking her life to any man. The models of manhood she had encountered hadn't been so wonderful and her highly free spirit aspired to something more than settling her life in a marriage, like all the rest of the womenfolk around her seemed to dream about.

And now look what was going on. A perfect stranger was descending on her life like a raptor from above, spoiling her projects, upsetting her family life. Someone who 'needed' her simply to avoid a legal problem, and so there she was - turned into a pawn to accomplish a mere need of a grotesque, almost frightening man who lived as though he was already in a grave. What a scandalous event! She couldn't accept this. She couldn't accept her mother's unreserved submission to his plans. How dare she do that? If her sister would have accepted a similar situation as a privilege, it was not the same for herself and her mother knew it well. She was 'selling' her daughter, like their crops at the town market.

Angry tears filled her eyes and she recalled the glance Lord K had bestowed on her as he left their cottage, while she was still outside with Daphne - in her over-excited emotional condition she had turned her frowned face towards the roses, with her arms folded on her breast.

She didn't want to take her dinner that night and there she lay, her eyes directed to the ceiling, tears shedding abundantly on the blankets.'

MILADY'S ROOM

CHAPTER FIVE

TOWARDS A NEW LIFE

'E l'animose man del duca e pronte

Mi pinser tra le sepulture a lui (...).'

'And the fearless, prompt hands of my guide

thrust me betwixt the sepulchres towards him (...).'

Dante Alighieri, *Inferno*, X 37-38[2]

'She got up at the same time as usual, ready to go to the Phillips. Her mother knocked gently at her door and

---

[2] Translation by Leni Remedios.

stepped in.

"What are you going to do? Did you make up your mind, my little Page?" she whispered.

"Please, don't call me that! *He* does!"

She went on putting her books in the bag, highly irritated. Bachmeier had affected her mother also in her speech - Mary Ann, aware of the independent spirit of her daughter, had never dared call her *my little Page* or other pet names of the sort, until he had started to do so.

"It seems that I have no choice, why are you asking me this question?"

She watched her daughter inquisitively but at the same time with merciful eyes. She was on the point of telling her, "*You aren't obliged to accept his proposal, my child. You are free,*" when, while approaching the door, Page said unexpectedly, in a tone that wished to be apologetic, "I'm going to talk with the Phillips today, to inform them that I'm going to leave the job."

She left the room, under the eyes of an astonished Mary Ann.

On the stairs Page turned and asked her mother, who had remained stunned at the threshold, "Did he provide you with an approximate date for the wedding?"

"Within fifteen days," she answered as if in a trance.

"Fifteen days? Are you serious, mother?"

"One month at the latest."

Too fast. It was all going too fast.

During her journey she diverted a little and stopped by the graveyard. She remained there to contemplate her father's slab for a while, trying to grasp from him, a dead man's spirit, some rationale for the absurd course of her life as a living being. It would have never occurred if he was still alive. It would have never occurred if he had given up on his stupid addiction. What did he have to suggest to her about this circumstance now? What could he possibly have advised about that if his ghost had come out from the grave and revealed anything about the future, like Farinata degli Uberti did, uplifting himself from his sepulchre in Dante's *Inferno*?

"*Maybe you are the last one to ask for advice,*" she thought sarcastically and she went on her way.

But I think I sense some kind of perplexity in your faces, my dear friends'.

MacAllister's remarks had taken everybody by surprise. Mrs Wood was smiling quietly, as if she hadn't understood them, while Mr Reede the butcher was looking around for help, hoping that someone else would eventually say something sensible.

Peter gave a cough and dared to say, in a timid voice, 'We have probably all heard about Dante's Inferno, but not in all its details.'

'Oh I see,' exclaimed MacAllister, a flash of understanding enlightening his face.

'I beg your pardon, dear friends, it is not my intention to show off in front of you and in doing so create a sort of, let's say, barrier between us.'

'Oh no, Mr MacAllister, on the contrary, it is a pleasure!' Mr Reede hastened to comment enthusiastically, his cheeks reddening more and more. 'Don't ever think we simple folks don't appreciate what a man of letters like you is saying!'

'Mr Reede is so right!' Mrs Wood added, leaning forward on her stick. 'It is absolutely delightful to listen to your narrative, reported with such elegant and educated manners.'

'Oh, I am overwhelmed, thank you. I feel I don't deserve such praise,' MacAllister said, quite confused.

'So, would you please explain to us,' Peter cut in, 'who Fari…'

'Farinata degli Uberti? Oh well, he was one of the damned met by Dante in his fictional journey through Hell. He was one of the heretics. In this encounter with the poet, he rose from his tomb, starting an animated exchange with him about the political life in Florence and…'

'Did the damned have the ability to predict the future, then?' Peter interrupted again, impatiently.

'Good question, Peter,' MacAllister replied kindly, but in the meantime casting him a sharp glance. 'You are taking me back to Page and to her father's grave, as a possible source of answers about her destiny. The answer is yes. But - according to Dante - their vision and knowledge were faulty. I mean, they had some knowledge of the future, but no knowledge about the present.'

'That's intriguing, Mr MacAllister!' The young postman exclaimed excitedly. 'It might be the same for Lady Lavinia. You said that she had the power to foresee the future, so she might have a glimpse about the following months or years, but she probably couldn't figure out what was going on at the present time, exactly like the damned in Hell. That's why she was so furious, because her rage was coming out of insecurity and doubt!'

'Yes, the lad is right!' nodded Mr Reede and the others with one voice.

'He might be,' MacAllister replied cautiously. 'However, I urge you to keep in mind this - no matter how great Dante was, all these conjectures about the damned were coming exclusively from his own imagination, while here we are talking about real events that were happening in our neighbourhood. It is no use indulging too much in speculation. Remember that the reality might surprise you even more.'

Peter sat back humbly in his chair and the others became quiet.

'The Phillips were absolutely surprised on learning the news,' MacAllister resumed coldly.

"Oh, not again," Mrs Phillips sighed, alluding to the previous governess's sudden marriage.

It didn't take much for the news to arrive at Young Phillips' ears, who found himself not only surprised but even disappointed - how was it possible? It sounded almost outrageous.

Nobody had ever proposed to marry one of the Ashbys and everybody in town knew the reasons why. And now that he had set his eyes on Page Ashby, someone else had come forward. Who was this brave fellow who dared spoil his own plans? In his mind it was as if Page Ashby naturally *belonged* to him, from the very moment he had fallen in love with her. Any remote hypothesis of a hindrance to his plans was out of the question.

Therefore he approached her, waiting desperately for her by the stairs, with a face that displayed all the range of feelings mingling inside him. Right from the moment she had seen him from above she had understood that she ought to face this last effort. She hesitated and stopped, looking down on him and there started to grow within her an unusual, fresh feeling of pride. Soon there will be no more Young Phillips in her life and no more Constance Phillips to pay attention to. Enough of struggling with a whimsical child and a vain, conceited man who flattered himself as "poet" and was aiming to win her love as a trophy. She suffocated a smile but, when he vehemently asked when on earth she had planned to marry and in some way insinuated a falsity about that news, she couldn't help but answer back:

"How can you say that, Mr Phillips? After all you don't know anything about me."

On her way back home she diverted again, but this time she bypassed the slope on which the graveyard spread, with its stones that seemed almost to cling desperately to the hill, and proceeded till she reached a road edge from which she could contemplate Lastsight Hill. The profile of the house stood out against the still bright sky of the afternoon, imposing, almost ironical, as though its windows were blinking at her.

A cold shiver ran through her spine. She had already seen Lastsight Hill's mansion on the occasion of the ball, but now it seemed something totally different. Its sombre aspect terrified her but at the same time fascinated her. An odd mix of repulsion and curiosity cohabited within her and suddenly she retraced in her mind the gloomy profile of the master of the house. The image of him was now merging with his mansion's outline over the hill, in a dreamlike vision, and suddenly she grasped it - Lord K and his mansion were like a single entity. She was starting to experience towards the house the same disturbing and ambiguous feeling she was experiencing towards its master. How different and far his world was from her own - she was now mentally recreating the features and the corners of the cottage, the daily life she was leading there with her family, the cheerful voice of her sister while gossiping during her sewing and Gertrude's sharp comments in German. Lastly, the library. Yes, maybe there something could be found that was related to what was awaiting her in Lastsight Hill. The precious stillness, the silence, the contemplation and the idea that no matter what turmoil might happen outside, she could still go back inside there and find her way. She turned again towards the graveyard's hill and murmured "Now I know, father."

The ceremony was very brief, as he had requested.
"It is just a formality, no useless ostentation please," he had recommended.
It was not exactly what Mary Ann had wished for one of her daughters, but the mere thought of a life with no more struggles as a consequence of the wedding pushed her pride into the background.
It had been decided that it would be a civil marriage. It would keep any prier away and in any case Lord K would have never consented to a religious wedding.
The only ones witnessing the event were all the Ashbys, Gertrude, Mr Bachmeier, Mrs Haffelaw – Lord K's housekeeper – and I.
Honestly, instead of a marriage it looked like a surreal ritual. The leading roles both wore a stern countenance and the mayor's general disregard on uttering his formulas by heart - which surely were boring to him as he celebrated at least two or three marriages per day - contrasted with the overexcited Mary Ann, who couldn't help bursting into tears. Why she was crying - whether for joy on having finally sorted out her endless financial troubles, or in repenting for giving away her daughter in such a circumstance - nobody could ever tell.
The most probable hypothesis, as Page herself hazarded, was that a mix of all these feelings and maybe even more was struggling within her and the solemnity of the event – if we can call solemn a grotesque moment like that – had simply released them.
Once outside and going towards the coach in her white gown, Page Ashby realized maybe for the first time that it was not an act - it was reality and she was really leaving her family in order to be gobbled up by Lastsight Hill.

With a thrill she imagined the profile of the mansion, exactly as she had contemplated it on her way back from the Phillips evenings ago - her imagination oddly mingled with her memories and behind the mullioned windows that had blinked ironically at her she was now fancying the profile of a woman, a pale woman, whose whiteness was appalling. She thought intensely over that for a while and her memory went back to the night of the ball, when she had ventured to walk in the dark gardens following Young Phillips and had noticed a wan lady observing her from a window. Why was the profile of a gaunt servant now haunting her thoughts?

"Page. Page!" It was Donovan waking her up from her musing, shaking her arm and trying to get her attention. "Will you come back to visit us some day?"

It was the first time that Donovan Ashby, twelve years old, had shown his own private feelings and the fact had surprised him the first of all. Having understood he was definitely going to lose his favourite sister and that life at the cottage would never be the same as before, he couldn't withhold his tears and without waiting for the answer he gave Page a tight hug.'

CHAPTER SIX

THE HOUSE

'It wasn't the deep silence between them that made Page Ashby feel uneasy.

Actually it had been a blessing that he hadn't spoken at all during the journey by coach.

He was clever enough to understand that any word in a situation such as this would sound pointless or even stupid. And so the clatter of the hooves on the ground was the only sound accompanying them all along the way home.

Home.

Indeed it was the sight of the mansion upon their arrival that stirred uneasy presentiments within her. Once again, the imposing building stood in front of her as if for the first time and it looked like a big stone mother, her huge stairs – the main on the front and the two by the sides –

unravelling like three long tongues of an eerie ancient Indian deity. Its medieval tower stood against the grey sky like the arm lifted by the deity itself, its battlements being fingers of an open hand, exactly such as you may have seen in some representations of Shiva the Destroyer, in one of the volumes of the Encyclopaedia Britannica lying on the shelves of your typical British family.'

At these words Mr Reede, the butcher, exchanged a puzzled glance with Mr Toulson, the postmaster, who in turn cleared his throat. Once again MacAllister – whose refined and in a way naïve nature made him somehow detached from the reality of the villagers, though sympathetic with them - had this bizarre idea that an expensive copy of the Encyclopaedia Britannica was a priority for any family in the country, in the same way that he had assumed that everybody - no matter their level of education - would know Dante Alighieri and the Divine Comedy.

Mr Toulson, who was not a man of letters but in his own way was a man of the world and had accumulated some knowledge purely by means of his contact with customers of different backgrounds, hastened to add:

'For the ones who might not know, Shiva is a deity venerated in India by people of Hindu faith.'

'Exactly, well said, Mr Toulson,' MacAllister nodded, 'and this kind of deity, in particular, is associated with the forces of destruction and darkness, counterbalancing – in a sort of cosmic dance – the pure forces of light symbolized by Vishnu, another deity of the Hindu pantheon. If you ever have the chance to step into Lastsight Hill's library, you will notice Lord K's collection of sacred texts in Sanskrit, coming directly from our colonies in India, with astonishingly beautiful representations of the Hindu pantheon and naturally with English commentaries at their sides. You will see and read how these cosmic forces work altogether and that actually Shiva is not just the Lord of destruction as such, but rather the Lord of transformation, setting the path for the next creation.'

Nobody dared to admit having never heard about such exotic stories.

'But at any rate,' MacAllister carried on, 'what Lady Page saw at the time was exclusively the grim aspect of the spot and she couldn't help but prefigure her own bleak future in this discouraging context.

At the bottom of the stairs a servant was waiting, wearing long muddy gardening boots and holding a shovel in his hand. It was Cezary, Lord K's valet who, extremely faithful to the memory of Lady Lavinia, had refused to take part to the ceremony, but couldn't contain his curiosity and had come to see the "new mistress". But it was not curiosity alone that had led him over there - by displaying an openly hostile attitude, he meant to show her that she was unwelcome.

This awkward situation was luckily interrupted by the barking of Ishtar, who came towards them cheerfully, even if at first she had reduced her speed on seeing a stranger and had sniffed at her suspiciously. Then she allowed herself to be stroked by this new human being, who smelled nice and was supposed to be a friend – so her instinct suggested, as this lady had arrived there together with her master.

Ishtar stood there, a friendly appearance amid a sombre setting.

Page felt as if a bad spell was cast on her and a wave of desolation overwhelmed her - an intuition supported by a sadly grey sky crossed occasionally by black noisy crows - and she felt an immediate impulse to tear away her ridiculous white apparel. But fortunately, right in that moment, Mrs Haffelaw appeared on the threshold with a large smile. She had preceded them with a little carriage, to check that everything in the house was in order before their arrival. Her stout figure and her appearance reminded Page of someone familiar - Mrs Haffelaw looked like a more refined and at the same time a stricter duplication of Mary Ann Ashby.

"Milady!" She welcomed Page, going towards her down the stairs and her affability broke the bad spell of the moment.

It was suggested that they had a brief meal before changing their dress, in order to restore themselves after that long day.

During this first and last meal together, he finally spoke.

She was surprised and a little amazed on seeing that he looked uneasy and nervous, more than she had expected him to be in such a situation. After all they were having lunch in *his* house and she felt simply like a guest.

At the time I was sure I would always feel a guest here in Lastsight.

He was forcing himself to be formal, merely giving practical indications about what she could do and what she couldn't. It looked as though he was dictating in plain terms a list of tasks to one of his servants, the tone was the same.

"Apart from the west wing, where my rooms are, you can explore any part of the house."

"Am I allowed to go in the glasshouse?"

He paused for few seconds, chewing a piece of vegetable he had slowly brought to his mouth, swallowed and answered, staring at her.

"Of course."

They went on eating in silence. Suddenly Jane, a young servant, arrived to serve a portion of beef to "Lady Page", as she was addressed for the first time,

I had a thrill on hearing that - it was the second step to my final realization that what I was passing through was real and not a bad dream.

but the maid skipped the master.

"Are you alright, Milord?" she dared to ask him.

"Why are you asking me that?"

"You didn't get the meat."

He fumbled with his fork.

"I can't stand the idea of blood in my plate."

She kept fork and knife still in her hands.

At his words she had immediately gone back in her mind to a scene she had beheld several times during her life - her mother washing and chopping rabbit or chicken flesh, something Page had always refused to do. How self-confident her mother was in her task, showing no hesitation, no repulsion at all in handling all that slippery flesh, blood and entrails that were slipping continually from her hands. And yet she would have had good reason to delegate that awful task to someone else.

Mary Ann had lost two children.

They were still living in her womb when fate decided that their little hearts should stop.

It happened once before Page's birth and then before Donovan's birth.

Each time, Mary Ann had seen the midwife with the little lifeless corpse of her own child in her arms, still pulsating and warm. And each time, she had sworn that she wouldn't have children anymore, the burden of the babies' deaths being too heavy to allow her to pass through another pregnancy with a light heart.

But evidently vitality is stronger than any conscious certainty.

Sometimes an odd thought passed through Page's young mind - what if destiny had decided to take her in the place of one of those children?

Why was it so established that she had to take her own place in the world? What contribution was life expecting from her?

It was a very idle thought indeed, leading to nowhere in their very practical life, and the very moment it arose in her mind she chased it away, saving it for her own solitary moments, when all the housework was done, all the clothes mended, all the vegetables gathered and she eventually could escape through the hills with her books in her hands, finding a nice place under a tree, overlooking the moors, sharing her deepest thoughts and feelings with Nature and the poets whose books she had brought with her. Only they could really find her thoughts worthy. Because, in the enthusiasm of her youth, she found that only Nature with her inexorable laws and poets with their sensibility next to the gods could understand properly the mystery of Life and Death.

She often wondered whether her mother, always so busy inside the house, was ever thinking about her unborn children. "Of course she is thinking about her unborn children," was the answer that she gave to herself every single time.

Mary Ann's restless eyes, roving from the furniture to dust to Donovan's hair to comb and to the gowns to mend or anything requiring an action, were merely trying to find a way to keep her silent grief quiet.

Mary Ann never said a word about her lost children, never. And Page would have never asked about them.

All this crossed her mind within a few seconds and - reawakening from her reveries – she felt that Death had been a blessing for poor Lavinia, saved from grieving over her own child's loss. This bitter and loathsome task had been consigned to her living husband - the sad, pale man whom Page was staring at in front of her, refusing to have "*blood in his plate*".

"It doesn't mean you have to pick up my habits," he said, looking with perplexity at her while she was staring motionlessly at her plate.
"I do apologize, Milord. I think I am just tired, even to eat. If you don't mind I would like to go to my…"
He nodded quietly.
"One last word, Milady." He said while she was already approaching the exit. "Later on Miss Haffelaw will show you all the rooms and recesses of the house. Your rooms are in the east wing. For any problems or requests you will call for Mrs Haffelaw or your personal maid, Joanna. I remind you what I told you earlier and I mean to be extremely clear about this: please don't ever bother me, unless for extremely urgent communications. And don't ever go, for any reason, in the west wing.'
She bowed and went away thoughtfully.

She followed Mrs Haffelaw, who was leading her through the eastern stairs. The steps were covered by a thick carpet and the wooden banister was finely carved. The luxury given to the house by its previous owner had been maintained in these details. At one time climbed by groups of finely dressed ladies, the staircase looked now hollow and melancholic. Lady Page had known the stories about the good old times in Lastsight Hill since she was a child, like everyone else in the neighbourhood. She had learned the 'legend' about the two stairs leading to the bedrooms and now that she was actually there she felt how the present silence was contrasting with the loud womanly voices that used to haunt those walls. The portraits once hung by Lord Coventry had been replaced with countryside landscapes, flowers and dark-coated horses riding in the snow.

His misanthropy extended to banishing humanity even from the paintings.

As a matter of fact nowhere in the house was a human portrait to be seen. Just one portrait was exhibited, but Lady Page knew nothing about it and was supposed never to behold it.

She was shown her room. It was a very large and bright chamber, with a canopy bed, heavy wooden furniture and damask walls, but most of all a massive mahogany writing desk by the window.

"Milord bade me to add this desk to your room," said Miss Haffelaw. "I objected to this, pointing out that a writing desk in a lady's room is not at all appropriate. Besides, there are already two of them in the library. But he insisted on saying that you would be pleased by it. What can I say? After all, my job consists in supervising the household. I can give suggestions to Milord, maybe some little words of advice based on my experience, but eventually I have to carry out orders".

While saying this, the housekeeper was scrutinizing the new mistress's face in the hope of catching a sign of disapproval about her master's inappropriate choice. However, Lady Page replied that she was indeed pleased and advised Mrs Haffelaw not to remove it.

"How did he guess?" she thought. Such an attention made her

feel more comfortable in that huge, bleak house.

Mrs Haffelaw called for Joanna, a young, red-cheeked girl. "She will be your personal maid. See you in an hour by the hall, Milady."

Joanna helped her to undress and change. The maid was visibly palpitating and panting a little - probably this was her first day of employment at Lastsight. She attempted to brush Milady's hair.

"I will do it by myself," Lady Page said spontaneously.

She had been brushing her hair all her life long and only Daphne was allowed to help her from time to time. It was a daily ritual that, in a simple gesture, had strengthened the intimacy between the two sisters.

But she saw a cloud of terror on the maid's face, who blushed violently, keeping the brush still in her hand. Her face suggested that she had been given some tasks to accomplish - what if she wasn't going to do what she was told?

"It's alright, you can do it."

Lady Page had learned her first lesson: here she was supposed to respect the normal procedure and to cast her eagerness for independence, which could upset someone else's vision of things, aside.

Whilst Joanna was brushing her hair, Lady Page was musing about the pause of silence Lord K had observed on answering her question about the greenhouse during dinner time.

What if he didn't really mean to allow her to go in there? Perhaps he had conceded out of mere courtesy, in order to appear not as strict as he actually was.

She knew from Bachmeier that Lord K was very fond of gardening and had arranged all the plants of his glasshouse by himself. Nobody helped him in that and he would spend hours in there almost every day.

At the back of her mind there was the wicked legend reported by her young brother about Lord K's wife being buried in there, as well as her own nightmare about the pit in the ground and the unknown corpse in it. However, considering it a silly thought, she had refused to think about this again.

What about Lord K's rooms? They were in the west wing and she wasn't allowed to go there. The little imp inside her had been naturally wakened by his prohibition: to forbid doing something to Page Ashby – pardon, Lady Page - was an open invitation to break the rules. She was imagining the western part of the house as a world apart, like a chapel in which he was hiding himself, with servants only for him - mournful assistants devoted to silence, like the pale maid that she had seen at the window on the night of the ball and who had long since continued to haunt her own thoughts.

An hour later she was by the hall, in accordance with Mrs Haffelaw's instructions.

Would you be surprised if I told you that, out of this entire first tour through the house, the only thing that aroused Lady Page's attention was the library? Well, anyone would have been as amazed and nearly moved as she had actually been - it is a huge library indeed, divided into aisles by massive, tall shelves. You can't guess the number of books, even approximately - one's sight literally loses itself among the innumerable volumes of every size and colour.

Mrs Haffelaw was a very practical woman and she was obviously struck when she noticed tears at the corners of Lady Page's eyes.

"Are you all right, Milady? I suppose you're still tired."

"This is…breathtaking," she continued walking through the aisles, taking a volume here and there, smelling the hard covers and leafing through the pages.

"*Odd wife for an odd man,*" Mrs Haffelaw probably thought, shaking her head. But externally she went on with her practical instructions. "The fire here is lit late in the morning, but if you prefer to change arrangements you have just to tell me."

If Lord K had his own grave on the west wing, Lady Page decided that the library would be her own pleasing grave, where she would have passed most of her time in Lastsight Hill.

Perhaps, the stone mother - the Shiva-the-destroyer-like house - was not so bad after all.'

CHAPTER SEVEN

WHEN IT ALL BEGAN

'Four months later, April 1901.

Queen Victoria had died some months earlier, as had Friedrich Nietzsche – the herald of the death of God. With them all the certainties of a whole era were buried and the new century was following an irreversible process of modernism, from its first wails.

It was undeniable - motors and electric street lighting were becoming common in all the big cities all across Europe and things were changing rapidly following the pace of progress. Hereafter nothing would ever be the same as before and romantic philosophers had nothing else to do but sing their own swan song.

But here in Lastsight Hill time had stopped.

Lady Page was astonished in discovering how pleasing her new life was to her. She was and still is a solitary type and the silence and the isolation of her new mansion fitted perfectly her status of poet and her deep connection with Nature.

She used to have long walks in her beloved moors, at any time she wanted. She did not have to restrict herself to a few hours outdoors, because nobody was expecting her home for dinner. Sometimes she would carry a hamper with some food and her notebook, allowing her to indulge herself outdoors for a longer time.

Ishtar had become an inseparable companion during those excursions. Her canine smartness had immediately perceived a good-hearted core in the newly introduced tenant and she had become instantly affectionate to her, a fact that strangely enough had aroused contrasting feelings on her master's part - naturally amazed and pleased that Ishtar had the opportunity of a further friend, but equally and undeniably disturbed by a sense of loss and jealousy.

On his way back from the moors, instead of being welcomed by the barking of Ishtar and by her wagging tail, he often saw his dog walking by Lady Page's side, totally careless of him. He came and they left - that had become the routine. And when they came back home, Ishtar preferred to remain longer with her mistress, refusing to go to him.

Lady Page was obviously enjoying the library as well, enthralled by authors from all over the world - people whose names she had never heard. She was surprised by the extent of Lord K's culture and knowledge, which the vast range of his library revealed.

Even the nasty glances of a permanently silent Cezary didn't touch her. She simply ignored him, even if she felt upset when he was speaking to his master in their native language in her presence:

I ended my worries by thinking that he was nasty towards anyone, not only against me.

So what was harassing her was certainly not an unbearable solitude, not at all. It was rather a stinging thought at the back of her mind or a sombre cloud looming over her - the feeling that something hostile was expecting her in some shaded corner of the house. Something – or someone – was hidden in an ambush waiting for a moment of weakness. What was agitating her was not so clear, even to herself. Feelings are never clear, they are often a skein of threads in contradiction with each other.

Besides, there was a very basic human need. It was true that she was a solitary type, but although previously – when she was living in the cottage with her family - she had had to struggle to obtain a piece of solitude outdoors and had to resign unwillingly when it was time to go home, in the course of time the mere idea that after all "nobody was expecting her for dinner" began to make her feel a little miserable.

I started to think that it wasn't healthy for a lady of my age to enjoy solitude so much. I realized I was perhaps too lonely.

And then there was the ghostly presence of Milord, whom she had never dared to bother and who was stirring contrasting feelings inside her.

Every morning, at the same early time, she could hear a rustling noise among the leaves - she got up, sure to discern, after a while, the massive head of Melmoth emerging from under the trees that grew in front of the stables and the dark hair of his master alongside, holding the reins and walking silently towards the wild moors.

She observed them every day, as though in a sort of ritual

- a bizarre waking up. She was struck by the obstinacy of his mourning and by the consistency of his deeds, which resembled the monotonous life of an inmate.

They met very few times and by chance.

Afraid of bothering him, whenever she realized he was in a room she did her best to avoid him and to move smoothly into another one. She talked to him only if consulted and it happened quite rarely, when coincidences brought them to meet in the hallways or in the garden and forced them to get into formal conversations. Despite his self-confident appearance he seemed every time to be curiously awkward, as though the obligation of coming out of his mournful shell and entering into contact with human beings – even though for a while – was really an extraordinary effort for him, the result of which was an unusual clumsiness. He always looked in a rush, impatient to go and hide.

Restrained by a sort of reverence, she had never as yet dared to ask him questions and never attempted to explore the glasshouse, notwithstanding his concession.

She was developing a growing eagerness to talk to him, to inquire about his amazing knowledge and about his past. He was aware of her inquisitive mind, yet he was too entangled in his grief to dare opening up. It was such a waste not to enjoy the knowledge of such a wise man. But she was resolute in respecting his will.

He told me not to bother him.

Regarding the events that had occurred during the recent years in his native land, the subject was a taboo, and she knew that she was supposed to stay out of it.

Nevertheless, his figure fascinated her and yet every time she stumbled on him she couldn't utter a word.

He told me do not bother him.

There was a detail in particular that was puzzling her and she divined that it was linked in some way to his past. During her first four months in Lastsight Hill she had never met a servant whose features could resemble those of the woman she had seen at the window, during the night of the ball. She had made timid inquiries, asking Mrs Haffelaw about how many servants there were in the house, their names and so on. She had asked it pretending to be interested in the household management, as a mistress is supposed to be. What would Mrs Haffelaw have thought about her if she had revealed the real nature of her curiosity?

Well, the answer was that there were only eight employees in the house: the maids Lorraine, Jane and Joanna, the old cook Madelaine, Cezary, Neal – a lad who helped Cezary with the gardening and the stables - Mrs Haffelaw as housekeeper and me as administrator and adviser. Lady Page was informed that the staff had always been the same since Lord K's arrival, except for Joanna, who was hired as her own personal maid upon her arrival. Just for the extraordinary occasion of the ball another ten young men had been employed as valets, sent there by Lady Deville, but that was all.

Therefore, she had persuaded herself that the profile she had seen that night at the window was a mere figment of her imagination and, even if not entirely satisfied, she had decided not to go back to the subject any more.

She even cautiously tried to ask Mrs Haffelaw some questions related to Milord's life in his native land, but it was clear, from the evasiveness of her answers, that she had been instructed to be reserved. The formal kindness of the housekeeper had never been a genuine source of companionship to Milady, due to the difference of personality between them. At first enthusiastic on having finally a mistress to look after, Mrs Haffelaw had done her best to bestow on Milady her attention, but she soon realized with disappointment that her young mistress didn't have the same attitude and habits of all the other young ladies. She disdained sewing, for example, and was easily annoyed by chatting, behaviours that had surprised her considerably, having got the intelligence that her mistress was a brilliant dressmaker and as a consequence having thought to please her by sewing together before the fire. Then she noticed that Milady preferred the company either of the dog or of books to that of herself, passing most of her time in the library or bringing a volume with her to the moors. Often during the night she even caught Lady Page bent over the huge writing desk that her master had bid her to place in Lady Page's room.

Sometimes Joanna, during her morning tasks, found ink stains on the white bed linen, to her utter disappointment. My master reported to me later how many times - stumbling by chance on his wife - he had noticed that her fingertips were ink-stained.

After all these oddities, no wonder that a distance had been created between the housekeeper and her mistress and a solid intention grew, on the part of the first, to stick to her duties only. Therefore, Milady's sudden questions about Lord K's past and the west wing rooms roused her irritation and she made no effort to dissimulate it. She had received precise instructions regarding these issues and simply didn't want to get into trouble, nor did she intend to find herself in the middle of a conjugal dispute caused by her own lack of discretion. So Lady Page lost her only source of company and even if she wasn't particularly fond of Mrs Haffelaw for the reasons I explained, she felt as though a heavy emptiness was growing inside her - the only one who had bestowed on her some kind words was now cold to her and the only one she really wanted to speak to was wrapped in his own halo of isolation which she didn't dare to break. Besides, the pleasure she was indulging in during her daily hours through the moors or in the silence of the library faded away during night-time hours or on any occasion during which her presence of mind yielded to the unpredictable, winding paths of the unconscious.

Mrs Haffelaw quite often caught her asleep in the library armchair - she didn't dare to wake her up, just limiting herself to stirring the fire and to closing the door behind her as softly as she could.

I used to abandon myself to the pleasure of the warmth of the fire and to the silence of the place. My limbs were still shaking after the long walks outdoors and I felt my eyelids heavier and heavier. I knew that gradually I would have slipped into the delight of a reposing slumber, but in the meantime a part of me was waiting anxiously and with a strange sort of excitement. As frequently happens I had a recurring dream - a nightmare – that had persecuted me since I was still in the cottage with my family (a pit in the ground, among the plants of the glasshouse, had come back to visit me many times, in many variations and disguises). Once I perceived Cezary lying down in the pit, but he wasn't dead - as I approached he opened his eyes and gave me one of his nasty glances; once I saw a little corpse that resembled the body of a little animal, maybe a bird or a rabbit and suddenly, behind my shoulder, I had heard Lord K uttering 'I can't stand the idea of blood in my plate'. Every time I closed my eyes I knew I had a sort of appointment and I was waiting in fear and in the most eager curiosity. I was certain that sooner or later she – the woman at the window – would come and visit me.

When solitude and misgivings reached a point of being unbearable even for her, she just called for a coach and went to visit her family.

She was glad to see that despite turning to a wealthy and comfortable life, her family had not lost control. Donovan was wild as ever, keeping on stealing stepping stones from the brooks, hiding them in the hem of his brand new shirts and dropping them on the endless path of the front garden. Her mother and sister had kept the habit of sewing, not because they needed to do so (they had obviously concluded at once the commitment with the Alans and their clothes shop) but just for leisure and because sewing encouraged their conversation. She smiled when on one occasion Mary Ann had whispered in her ear something like "You know what? For the first time in my life I have experienced what it means to be bored. Boredom is for wealthy people." She simply did not have to accomplish all the tasks she needed to do before.

Lord K had provided two other servants to support Gertrude. The latter was at first upset by this intrusion, but soon the new maids – two young local ladies – had learned how to soften Gertrude's hard temper and presently they were singing German folks tunes together while hanging the laundry, laughing aloud at the unavoidable mistakes of pronunciation of the English girls.

Lady Page considered these visits to her family a "salutary break", a "step back to reality".

But she would have never come back to live with them. After a few hours of chats with Daphne, laughter with Donovan and remarks to Mary Ann, she felt it was enough and she ardently desired to go back to her lair.

It was a mysterious, uncanny spell. It was the appeal that Lastsight Hill exercised upon her.'

'Did you ever speak to her?' The shrill voice of Peter woke everyone up from the daydream.

'Do you mean at this time? No, at the time I wasn't as familiar with Lady Page as I later became. As I told you, she really respected his will not to be bothered and she associated my person with yet more issues in which she wasn't allowed to involve herself. So every time I arrived I often perceived the back of her gown sweeping across the floor and her figure disappearing in another room. Sometimes, very rarely, our eyes met and I divined in her glances a hard desire to know something from me, but we never had occasion to talk alone. I have to say it wasn't mere curiosity in her countenance - I can't explain how, but I understood that I had in front of me a woman radically different from the young ladies that I had occasion to meet. Well, she hadn't run away from that mansion yet, as any other lady of her age and status would have done - I told you how Lord K had become really grumpy and it was a mystery how she could bear to live in a lonely and desolate place like Lastsight with such an unsociable man. Though I had access to a good amount of his confidence, Lord K's inaccessibility was overwhelming. No one could have possibly broken it, not even I.

His most intimate core was reserved to the one in the west wing, only to her, preserved and untouched by the rest of human society.

Observing Lady Page from the outside I had this strong feeling that somehow she was going to breach his inaccessibility and honestly I wasn't sure that this would have brought any good to her.

He was poised on the edge of insanity. He stood right between the realm of reality - where things had their proper name and meaning - and a distorted realm, where things were either a dangerous menace to his peace or a sad reference to one of his memories. Just a matter of a light, unperceivable push and he would have suddenly fallen from the edge, right into the deepest of the gorges.

I had the strong sensation that Lady Page alone could provide the hook that would have held him tightly on the edge and would have prevented Lord K from falling miserably down.

It happened on a clear sunny morning of April, a typical early spring day. The air was fresh but promising heat for the succeeding hours. Very few clouds were discernible on the horizon.

Lady Page thought it was a waste remaining indoors with such a nice weather and so she took a book with her – a collection of the Brownings' poems – and went into the front garden. She was not intending to walk long distances for the moment, so she kept roaming about the garden for a while, holding her book in her hands. Without realizing it she had stumbled on the benches of the arbour. She had never been moved by any kind of emotion at the sight of the arbour, having easily forgotten about the incident of Young Phillips and Lady Deville. If anything of that event still haunted her subconscious, it was the woman at the window, even if her rational part had put an end to this worry. She instinctively gave a glance towards the window by the west wing and then finally sat down. The blighted creeping ivy had been finally removed and the sun beams arrived unobstructed to her face. She was delighted by the warmth of the first spring sun on her skin. The air was faint with the sweet odour coming from the jasmine shrubs that had been planted on the south side; it merged and melted with the strong smell coming from the massive, nearly monstrous rose bush by the northern bench. The majestic size of the latter made it look like an old defiant giant compared with the shy, recently planted jasmine. Cezary was trimming shrubs in the distance and the noise of the scissors trimming the leaves came to her ears regularly. Sparkles of sunlight on the smoothed animal statues, now cleaned as if brand new, hit her eyes. She felt dizzy, pleasantly dizzy and lost her sense of reality. The lines on the book melted. She closed her eyes, enjoying that sweet loss of consciousness.

It lasted a few minutes. A strong blast suddenly struck her person, madly turning the pages of the book on her lap. She opened her eyes and realized that all around her the trees and the shrubs had begun to bend violently. Cezary had stopped trimming.

It had been all of a sudden.

"Typical unpredictable spring weather," she thought with no alarm and as she got up the shape of the glasshouse stood imposingly in front of her. She had never ventured in. What better occasion? She approached the entrance, unaware that she was going to have one of the strongest supernatural experiences of her whole life.

Silence inside. All around her, outside the shell of the glasshouse, trees and bushes were tossed wildly by the fury of the wind. The long grass blades were waving like the surface of a stormy sea. It was uncanny and fascinating at the same time - the mute vision of furious Nature, every sound being hushed by the thick glass of the building. It was like lying in the stomach of a huge clam, well protected from the dangers of the wild abyss. She leant her book on a shelf nearby - how could she resist the temptation of contemplating the marvellous sight out there? A metal sound behind her woke her attention - it came from the door. She discovered that the door was locked, as if someone had locked it from the outside.

She tried to force the handle, but there was nothing to be done. She turned and in the distance perceived Cezary going towards the house with his tools - she knocked hard, calling him loudly but he couldn't hear her - the wind was too noisy and she was inside. He went on his way towards the mansion, holding his hat tightly on his head.

It couldn't be him, impossible, however nasty he was. Besides, he was too far away to have shut the door at the time it had happened.

But all of a sudden her attention was drawn from Cezary to something up in the sky: a black smudge, it seemed, most probably a cloud. Its hasty movements were however too strange to be attributed to a cloud. What was it?

"For God's sake, what is it?" she murmured to herself.

The answer was soon given, as the cloud approached closer and closer - dozens, hundreds of crows, all close to each other, were moving together, towards...towards her. That was clear, from the first instant - they were coming *for her*. No doubt about it at all. Even now she can't explain how this certainty came to her so clearly.

They were flying almost above Lastsight when they parted in groups and started to fly in circles right above the glasshouse. She looked around her, terrified. No help could come from the cheerful lemon trees or from the funny tall cactus, that now seemed to mock her devilishly - plants were part of Nature, exactly like the crows out there, and they had transferred their allegiance to the birds.

They went on flying in circles for a long time, maybe one hour, till her nerves became exhausted. From time to time one of them parted from the group and nose-dived towards the glasshouse. It would slam against the panel, slip down to the ground and, after limping a few steps, would rise up again as if nothing had happened, joining the flock. She couldn't hear the flapping of their wings - the sound came to her rather muffled by the thick glass. So the hordes of black birds, wreathed in silence, were a most dreadful sight.

Then some individuals simply perched and started tapping frenetically on the panels.

What could she do? There was no way out, every attempt at running away was impossible and even if she succeeded it would be useless - they would have caught her at once.

"Why?" she thought, "why has Nature revolted so angrily against me?"

Too horrified and aghast to break into tears, she kept her eyes wide open in an incredulous strain of attention.

Then she saw *her*.

Among the black feathered bodies flying around the glass house, she discerned a sort of white spot, surrounded by a window's frame - it was the same pale woman whom she had perceived that night. A hint of triumph pervaded Lady Page, even in the middle of such dramatic circumstances - it wasn't a figment of her imagination! She was there and she was real, staring dreadfully at her.

"It is you. *You* did it," Lady Page whispered. "You didn't visit me in my dreams; you came to visit me for real."

As she uttered these words a clamour was heard, a sound coming from the hysterical flapping of hundreds of wings - from the groups in which they were flying around, they had all suddenly flown down and reunited, flocking on the top of the glasshouse. From the outside it looked as if a giant creature had laid a black feathered blanket over the building.

She didn't like it. She didn't like it at all. This sudden stillness – none of them was tapping now – was far more frightening than the sight of them flying in circles.

Rows of beaks and wild dark eyes surrounded her. All silent, all still.

Suddenly one started to caw. Then a second one and a third. After a while all the flock of crows was cawing and she had to press her hands on her ears not to be driven mad by the hideous noise, which seemed to pierce the thick panels.

Then they rose up again, fluttering together - this time they looked bolder and were individually swooping down with much more fury than before, like little black fiends. *Bump!Bump!* Their intent was clear and she desperately resigned herself to her fate - they meant to draw her eyes out of her body, to grasp her hair, to jab at her hands and face.

The glass panels were by now cracking under the continuous bumps of the birds and finally one of them crashed down, leaving on the glass rim a frame of blood and black feathers. The wounded little body fell down with a noisy tumble on the ground, among the berries. The glass had shattered asunder. Some shards hit Page's arms and her hands, which she had put over her head in the attempt to protect herself. The little black fiend's wing went on jerking for a while. But what she had tragically foreseen didn't happen - the other birds, instead of taking advantage of the crack in the glass to get in, flew away all at once, as if frightened by something. She couldn't have heard it but - at the same moment in which the bird had crashed through the glass and had fallen down - another crash was made at the door. It had been caused by an axe being thrown through it.

Fits of pain all along her arms. And the unbearable, gruesome feeling of a paralyzed body - she felt her eyelids heavy like concrete and her limbs incapable of moving. Out of nowhere a giant, black feathered head came towards her, steadily. Its beak was horribly long and drenched with gore. Yes, it was happening: she felt a painful pang on her right arm and in an instant she was aware of her flesh being eaten up. However much she tried to scream out her pain, her mouth simply didn't open and her voice remained distressfully suffocated within.

Desperation suddenly gave way to resignation.

"You win."

The whisper had come deep from inside her, as though it was her last death-rattle, clinging awkwardly in her throat.

"What?"

A chink in the dark wall of her concrete eyes cracked.

"What did you say, Milady?"

The voice was calm and soft. The chink enlarged and in front of her she could gradually perceive the black feathered-like head of Lord K.

After all the strain of her mind during that horrible event and after the sight of Lord K coming into the glasshouse with an axe in his hands, she had fainted.

She was presently lying on the big armchair where he usually sat before bedtime. In her half-sleep she was feeling soft fingers poking her skin but her delirious state – fuelled by exhaustion – was turning mere physical feelings into the bites of a ravenous crow.

He was kneeling in front of her, his sleeves rolled up, his dark hair dangling before his eyes, hiding partially the sight of her. She perceived pieces of white cotton lint around her arms. Wounds still not treated were under his attention. He was cleaning and disinfecting them carefully. His pale thin fingers were moving on her skin with the precision of a clockmaker. She had forgotten that he was a doctor.

He had bound her arms to the armchair with some other cotton cloth in order to keep them still and in such a way as to keep her hands free to move, so that he could attend to all her fingers. She could observe him at a very close quarters.

"I dreamt about the crows."

"I see."

"And about you."

The clock was ticking the time noisily.

"You were a huge specimen of a human crow eating up my arms."

"Well," he proceeded with her fingers now, apparently unmoved by her words, "I dare say that what you have been through was enough, no need of further nightmares."

"Indeed."

They remained silent for a while. She was scrutinizing him in a different way now. She was coming to her senses and tried gradually to reconstruct the events she had gone through more rationally.

"Why did you lock yourself in?" he asked abruptly, without looking at her.

"I didn't."

"I couldn't open the door from outside. It was locked from the inside."

She grew uneasy.

"I didn't."

They looked at each other. Something ran instantaneously between their minds, a quick intuition, like a shudder along the spine.

"I suppose the door must have slammed close with the strong wind then," he said finally.

It was the formal conclusion that was supposed to put an end to the issue.

"Probably the lock had been damaged. I will call for a smith to check it."

The voice whispering inside her was choking.

I saw her.

"You were lucky, Milady."

I saw her.

"Yes, I was," she said laconically. And, weirdly enough, she felt her strength coming back abruptly, along with a sense of impertinence.
"It was an extraordinary coincidence that you were around at the moment it happened."
He suddenly lifted his head and stared at her.

*I think some kind of bravery in my tone had struck him. Well, he had just insinuated that I had locked the glasshouse door by myself, as if I was seeking attention. It was the very first time that we were talking so closely, if you exclude all the cold formalities whenever we had met in the house or in the gardens. I wasn't familiar with him, therefore at that moment I couldn't give a correct interpretation of his frown - soon he lowered his eyes again and enlarged them for a while, his lips extremely clenched, his breathing growing faster. I felt uncomfortable, bound as I was to the armchair, unable to move, some of my wounds still open and aching and he…he was confusing me with his attitude. What was passing through his mind? Was he musing on the fact that I had laid a sort of accusation against him? Was he thinking about that woman? Was he merely worried about the possibility I could have seen her? Because at that point I was more than suspecting the existence of such a woman: I was **sure** that she was real. In one way or another. And I was deeply convinced that her presence was linked to Lord K, that he wanted to keep her presence secret and had instructed all the servants – Mrs Haffelaw first – not to give any information about that, in a sort of silent complicity that kept all the inhabitants of the house coalesced* *against me. It wasn't difficult to understand who the woman might be. In the deep of my heart I knew. But my mind was seeking desperately a rational explanation and wasn't ready yet to admit any hypothesis which might transgress the line of plausibility. He gradually recomposed himself and gazed at me again. The cool manner with which he answered me left me even more confused.*

"It wasn't coincidence." He said in a dry voice, "I was walking as usual on the moors when suddenly Melmoth stamped his legs and refused to go on. He shook his head; his legs were like stuck in the ground. He was trying to tell me to go back."
Lady Page looked at him attentively.
"Then I heard it."
He went on healing her wounds.
"You heard what?"
"Their terrible noise. I looked around and I noticed a huge flock of black birds flying madly above Lastsight Hill. In the meantime, the wind had started to blow furiously - I thought that a storm was going to arrive soon, the kind of storm that makes animals restless and nervous, like before an earthquake. It's the only explanation I can give of the birds' behaviour and of Melmoth's stubbornness."
He didn't speak anymore.

Is that all? Is that how he explains what happened?

"So I came back and that's how I found you."

I saw her.

She didn't utter a further word and he proceeded to heal her hands under her inquisitive eyes.'

CHAPTER EIGHT

THE PORTRAIT

'Another dream disturbed her sleep that night. This time it wasn't the pit in the glasshouse. This time ravens went on flapping their wings during Lady Page's slumber, as if in reality they had never gone away. They weren't persecuting her, it was rather the opposite - they gave her a sort of call and their voices made her get up from her bed and go out of her chamber. She went downstairs to the hall but the sound seemed to be coming from somewhere upstairs. She lifted her eyes and a crow was perched alone on the big chandelier. The gleams of the innumerable crystals disturbed her eyes and she screened them with her hand. As soon as she lowered her hand the hall suddenly became full of dancing couples, all of them dressed up in gorgeous attires, like they were during the night of the ball.

In a moment the crow flew towards her, grazed her hair

and took to the direction of the staircase. Not the main staircase, but the forbidden one, the one leading to the west wing. The bird stood by the banister, cawing noisily, as if inviting her to follow it. She followed it. The stairs were grey and bare. They had nothing of the magnificence of the ones in the east wing. She proceeded slowly, keeping her hand on the banister. But then she realized that nothing was under her hand - the banister had vanished and she found herself on the edge, nearly on the point of falling down into the stairwell. Then she heard a loud caw by her side and felt a hand strongly grasping her arm.

I told you not to bother me.

The face of Lord K appeared quite close to hers, in a desperate, grim countenance. Copious tears shed from his eyes and all of a sudden all the other crows came out from a chamber that was at the top of the stairs, flapping noisily around them both. At this point Lady Page awoke.

She was unable to rest her mind and waited anxiously for the dawn. This last dream had once more agitated her and she spent all the remaining hours of the night musing about what she had experienced lately. An appalling doubt was haunting her in particular - was Lord K actually colluding in this woman's intent? After all, he had obtained what he wanted with the marriage and he didn't need her anymore. Were they both trying to frighten her on purpose, to get rid of her? That was impossible, why should he do something like that? She was discreet as she had been requested to be; she had never bothered him and had never given him the opportunity to blame her for not having followed his instructions. He was frank and sincere - if something about her attitude had disturbed him he would have told her.

But then her chain of suspicions led to a spiral of preposterous thoughts that was escalating more and more. Maybe the awkward countenance that he was displaying every time they met and his evasiveness on the night of the birds' incident – she thought - could be explained by his feeling bad about his scheming against her.

Her utmost perplexity, united with an unavoidable curiosity, was leading her towards a decision: to break the rules and explore the west wing. It was manifest that the answer to all her perplexities lay over there and her last nightmare was an open invitation to trespass the forbidden limits.

The first beams of the morning sun touched her skin and the bound wounds on her arms.

She heard the rustling of the leaves - she got up, approached the window and after a while, as usual, perceived the dark figure of Lord K, walking with Melmoth by his side.

She put a shawl on her shoulders and went out of her room. It was too early to see Joanna around - she was supposed to wake her lady up in an hour and at this time of the day Mrs Haffelaw was giving the cook instructions about the meals, while Cezary and Neal were busy by the stables after Milord had left for the moors.

So upstairs was silent and deserted, nobody could see her. The problem was that she had to go downstairs first, in order to take the other staircase leading to the west wing. She descended the stairs still in bare feet, listening attentively to every possible sound or voice, but everyone was busy in other rooms.

She gazed suspiciously at the big chandelier, remembering her dismal dream. How many times it had frighteningly swung under a sudden blast coming from an open window.

On those occasions Mrs Haffelaw would hastily arrive to shut the window up, murmuring something against *"the wind of the moors"*. The wild wind of these regions is a constant presence, as you know. Lady Page loved it. She remembered staying in her father's library, almost holding her breath for fear and ecstasy on listening to the rumbling of the wind, how it shook the casements and the entire cottage. Now she was linking the wildness of the wind to the grim appearance of the crows that had attempted to attack her.

She took a passage that led to the north side of the house, hugging the kitchen wall. Mrs Haffelaw's voice was complaining about Lord K's habit of avoiding meat and about her trouble finding some good alternatives for him to eat. She expressed also her incredulity about how he had passed on his habit to Milady as well. Lady Page restrained a chuckle and her curiosity would have kept her there to listen further, were it not for her awareness of her specific purpose. So she went on and, after having crept around the mansion's recesses a little, she found herself at the foot of the staircase. She shivered at its sight - it was exactly as it was in her dream. She climbed the stairs, walked along the landing and at the bottom of the dark hallway she found the door she had dreamt about - she walked directly towards it, with no hesitation. She put her trembling hand on the door handle, as if wondering about the flock of black birds that had come out from it. A sudden impulse to run back to her room was trying to prevail now. Eventually she decided to open the door and found herself in the deepest darkness of a gloomy room. The shutters were closed and she didn't dare to open them, afraid as she was to raise a suspicion. Gradually her sight adjusted and began to discern the outline of the objects and she almost gave a shriek on perceiving the bulk of a mannequin, which she had mistaken for a human figure. She touched it and felt the softness of a silken shawl. Her own figure was slightly visible in the mirror of the dressing table and she sat down for a while in front of it, surprised and amazed by the sight of womanly stuff like brushes, ribbons and a necklace of fine white pearls. She caressed the brushes' bristles and, as if caught by a sudden spell, remained like this for a good while, till the noise of some steps woke her. She got up in panic and walked around seeking a place to hide in, till she stumbled on some long draperies in her way. She hid behind them and waited, holding her breath.

Someone entered in with heavy, noisy steps. The old wooden shutters creaked - a first sunbeam entered and the darkness of the room was scattered, as if the myriads of black birds had really flown away, yielding room to the daylight.

In her deepest consternation she noticed that the person who had entered was Cezary.

Obviously she had no idea that he was in charge of checking and cleaning that room and thought he was busy in the stables with Neal. But he had left the boy to his occupation and had come upstairs for his daily survey and to give a breath of fresh air to the rooms.

This was not the biggest surprise.

She was startled when the sunbeams gradually illuminated the real occupant of the room - from above the fire's mantelpiece a proud pale face was staring at her, the face that she had always mused about. From behind the draperies, holding the material tightly as if for fear of falling from a cliff, Lady Page was stunned in the contemplation of the only human portrait she had ever observed in the house - she was facing the rival whose existence she had always suspected from the depth of her heart. She was facing Lady Lavinia.

Luckily Cezary went out soon after having opened the windows. She waited and, hearing that the noise of the steps was fading away, ventured out from her hiding place towards the fireplace. She lifted her eyes and contemplated better the beautiful, majestic woman in the portrait, who wore a dark frock, exactly like Lady Page herself used to wear while working as a governess. Nevertheless, her countenance was that of a lady of noble rank. Her slightly raised smile revealed a strict temper and at the same time a veiled soft core. Her dark hair was neatly tied at the nape and the only one ornament on her was a white pearl necklace, the very same that Lady Page had found on the dressing table. A mixture of awe and tenderness arose in her and instinctively she lowered her eyes, as if the stern eyes she was in front of were real and did not belong to a portrait - she felt like the humble jasmine shrub by the arbour, facing the giant rose bush.

She caught the reflection of her own silhouette in the mirror and felt a sense of repulsion at the sight of it. She looked at her bare feet, at her plain nightgown and at her loose hair and concluded that the clumsy young lady in the mirror could never be compared to the self-confident woman of the portrait.

The lady in front of her was strong and fierce.

She - the small shivering thing underneath - was vulnerable and insignificant.

She could scarcely move, as if a sudden movement of hers could have the power to upset the portrait and the absurdity of her supposition didn't help her. But then a detail diverted her attention: a solitary notebook that lay on a little desk, with a pen at its side. An irresistible curiosity led her to read the lines that someone's hand had traced on the leaves inside - lying there, undoubtedly, was the answer to all her misgivings.

Slowly she tiptoed towards the desk, as if afraid of awakening some sort of entities. She opened the black hard cover of the notebook and started to peruse it. She gave a quick glance to the portrait every now and then, sure that her act of perusing the notebook was in some way unnerving her rival. She felt the weight of her dark eyes on her, but was set on going on regardless.

"After all it's just a portrait." It was the internal deceitful voice of reason that reassured her.

The pages were deeply filled with a thick and neat handwriting. Each page reported the date on which the note was written. The tone was that of a personal collection of very intimate reflections. She felt scandalously guilty for what she was doing, but couldn't help going on - the fluidity of the black ink was leading her eyes bewitchingly, while the tenderness of the words was capturing her deepest emotions.

Quite often the notes left the prose to follow a sudden rhythm similar to poetry, resulting in a strange mixture between them. Sometimes quotations were interposed among the author's reflections. Less often a poem in blank verse appeared.

"October the 4th 1898.
When the fogs descend on the moor and the hill peaks around me hide from my sight,
Then I take my horse and, walking with him by my side,
I venture through the hills wrapped in the fog.
My cold heart appears to be healed by the tender mist;
In that it finds a relief, a shelter, a balm for its own wounds.
It seems that it fits perfectly with this remote, gloomy ingle of the good old England.

While the sunny days' mirth, that reveals the truth upon everything,
Pricks my heart like the sharp point of a diamond.
In the thickest mist it's guarded my woe.
In the thickest mist I can hide my silent tears.
Like gems in a jewel box."

"April the 21st 1899.
Not a sound
But the sound of Thee
When all the notes collapse
I'll finally reach you
When all the noises implode
I'll finally join you
When all the tears dry
And return back to the eyes yet cold
Like the waters of a brook
Going upwards back to the glacier
Upon the soundless mountain peak
Then, just then
I'll allow my ears to be fulfilled
By the rumbling of your stillness
By the glacial notes of your
Endless silence."

"November the 16th 1900.
Cold is the earth[3]
...and cold is my heart..."

The profundity of the feelings expressed in those leaves;
the dignity of the grief that they conveyed; the sense of her
absolute impotence in front of the vastness of sorrow - all
this was overwhelming her with an emotional wave that

---

[3] From the poem *Remembrance*, by Emily Brontë.

she had never experienced in her young life and she could hardly breathe, as though a nameless weight was oppressing her bosom.

In turning over the pages with her shivering hands she realized an apparently meaningless detail: the frequency of the notes was lessening with time. Until, by about the end of December, they incredibly disappeared. The last note, quite different in both tone and shortness, was a unique, repeatedly written sentence and the handwriting, a far cry from the neat lines of the beginning, was uncertain and tremulous:

"Don't blame me".

Don't blame me. She mentally repeated. These last words echoed in her mind obsessively. She mused on that and started at the thought that December 1900, when the notes were beginning to diminish, was exactly the time by which she had arrived at Lastsight Hill.
She lifted her eyes. She had the feeling that someone had caught her thoughts.
It was then that she felt it. The terrible stench that had filled my nostrils every single time I had trespassed that room on the west wing, was now pervading Lady Page, almost attacking her like a predator - the smell of blood. It hadn't appeared before, as if hidden in ambush, waiting for the right moment to enwrap its prey and subsume her, like a smart winding boa.

A sudden warmth between her legs startled her - her immaculate nightgown was stained red in her lap. The stain was growing larger and larger, like a red ink blotch, as though an invisible hand had on purpose spilled a red ink bottle over a perfectly white leaf.

While her reason was striving towards a plausible explanation, her forces faded and she fell down to the floor, finding her own hands and the gauzes on her lower arms tangled in the dense fluid.

Her consciousness was abandoning her. She was gradually passing the threshold of a dimension where the borders of time and space were blurring. An incredible fit of pain rose from her lap and she uttered an acute shriek.

She opened her eyes and found herself lying in a large bed. Panting faces were busy around her. She was able to see in particular three women, wearing blood-stained aprons - one of them was pressing her stomach. The other two were by her feet. And that indescribable pain again arrived with a stronger pang and with it an obscure certainty - the thing that had been drawn off her womb was not alive, not any longer.

The hands of a fourth person were holding her by her shoulders and caressing her hair now and then. They were manly hands. She lifted her head and her last sight before exhaling her final breath was the sobbing face of Lord K.

She reopened her eyes.

The first object her consciousness had to deal with was the portrait - the sparkle of tenderness that Lady Page had believed she had detected in it had completely disappeared, making way for mere pride and malignity. Her trembling hands ran instinctively across her lap and found it perfectly clean and dry.

She finally got up and contemplated her once again immaculate nightgown. Shivering and wavering she went out of the room, completely haggard and exhausted by the devastating power of the hallucination.

Donovan was playing distractedly at the piano with one hand, his head resting on the other one. The notes interweaved with the acute sounds of the chickens being chased by the dog in the back yard and with the noise of the servants stowing the cutlery in the kitchen. The result was strangely soothing to the ears. But the domestic quiet of a Sunday afternoon in the Ashbys' cottage was a prelude to the melancholy of dusk and to the torments of the night. Something disruptive was in the air.

The symphony of sounds was interrupted by Bachmeier's voice.

"You look thoughtful, Mrs Ashby."

She wouldn't answer immediately. She sighed and drew the curtains aside, avoiding her friend's eyes.

"I wonder how Page is over there," she finally said, struggling to control her emotions.

"I am sure she is fine," Mr Bachmeier reassured her. "Last time that she visited you she looked so serene."

"I am afraid she is not serene at all. She is resigned, that's all she is. Sir," she eventually turned and looked straight into his eyes, "have I done the right thing?"

"Of course you have!" he said emphatically.

Donovan stopped playing the piano.

"Carry on playing, boy, it's nothing, we are simply discussing. You are gifted, by the way. Carry on. Regret is pointless, my dear lady," he added, turning again towards Mary Anne. "Its only use is to destroy the present, or - better said - to project onto our lives an option of a future that we will never know. Will you allow it to destroy your present?"

"It's not about my present, sir, it's about hers."

"Too late." It was Donovan talking. He had started playing the piano again. His fingers flew over the keys with growing vivacity; his spine was straight and his mind quite alert. Adults keep forgetting that young lads like him are not toddlers any more and they are not indifferent to adults' conversations. And in this particular case the subject was dear to him. Nobody had ever asked him how he felt about the whole situation with his sister. That was apparently how it worked with grown-ups: they take decisions and - whatever they are - you have to accept them. Furthermore, they assume that you are not only going to accept it, you are going to accept it unquestioningly, as though it was the most natural thing to do. To them he didn't have an opinion and if he had one it didn't matter.

He missed his sister. He had always been surrounded by women since he was a little child, but at least with Page he was able to establish a kind of complicity that nobody else was ever able to offer him. He had nothing in common with Daphne, his mother annoyed him and he didn't like his mother's friend. Well of course, Page didn't like Mr Bachmeier, therefore it was a logical consequence that he didn't like him either. The gentleman had told him that he was gifted at the piano only to keep him quiet. He had never cared about a young lad like him. Nobody cared but his sister, who was now unhappy, living alone in a grim house on the top of a hill with a lunatic. All this to please their mother's will. And for what? For new linen in the cupboard, a couple of noisy servants and for paying off a debt that they would have paid off anyway sooner or later. He had kept all these considerations to himself so far. Hence his words caught them by surprise. They were just two words. *Too late.* They both decided to ignore him nevertheless and to carry on their conversation as if he wasn't there, while he carried on playing as if he had said nothing. His fingers were talking in his place, nervously pressing the piano keys with growing passion.

"She was quite happy about that at the time, actually she accepted it," Bachmeier went on.

"She felt compelled to do so," Mary Anne added vigorously, "and when someone feels compelled to do something there is no room for happiness."

The piano music was louder and louder.

"Mrs Ashby, you have done your best."

But again she wouldn't listen.

"What have I done?" She kept saying shaking her head. "What have I done?"

A huge bang was heard and along with that the roaring echo of the keyboard - Donovan had abruptly slammed the wooden lid down on it.

"You have bargained over Page's life for some wealth in return," he shouted in fury before taking the stairs three steps at the time.

Mary Anne was shocked. She had never seen Donovan so upset before.

"You see?" she cried aloud. "We are supposed to be happy, yet we are not! I am not. Donovan is visibly not. The household is not the same.'"

'Well, the boy was right, it was a bit too late for regret, wasn't it?'

It was Peter's voice that interrupted McAllister's narrative. 'She was simply trying to do her best for her family, as Mr Bachmeier pointed out,' Mrs Wood exclaimed.

'Oh yes indeed, but I think she might have thought earlier about the consequences of her decisions about her daughter, if she really cared about her. Don't you find a bit of hypocrisy in all that? I mean, she always seemed to care more about social approval than Page's happiness.'

'You shouldn't be so harsh with your judgement,' the butcher interjected. 'You are still too young to understand

- let's discuss it again when you have your own family.'

In a minute the post office became hot with debate.

McAllister took advantage of the situation to enjoy some rest and quietly observe the animated discussion among the others. Mr Toulson, the postmaster, was struggling to calm them down.

'If I were you,' he eventually intervened, 'I would wait to hear more.'

He beckoned almost desperately to Mr McAllister, inviting him to carry on.

'Well, your discussion is very interesting nonetheless,' he said before resuming the story, 'and shows different sensibilities in such matters as human feelings and consequent behaviour. We will come back to the Ashby family, to Mary Anne's regret and Donovan's anger. But now, let's go back to Page's thoughts and to what she made of her last supernatural experience. What did Lady Lavinia want to demonstrate by making Lady Page relive her own experience of death and of giving birth to a dead child?

I reached the conclusion that she intended to make clear the nature of exclusiveness that her relationship with Lord K had, a tremendous tie of death and blood, that bound him to an unwholesome fidelity till the end of his life. It was easy for Lavinia: she was the stronger of the two, a strength derived from her belonging to a supernatural dimension; he was weak, a weakness derived from his condition as a mortal, tangled in his own skein of painful emotions and feelings, almost abandoned by his most lucid and rational faculties. She knew this perfectly and tried to get the most out of it. I was the intruder. I was the disruption. I was the one who was getting closer to him in some way and she was desperately trying to find the best way to get rid of me. Yes, I said desperately. She made me startle, she made me shiver, but she never managed to defeat me. Now I can fully explain to myself how, during all the time I spent in Lastsight Hill, I've never felt completely frightened by that woman and I've gone on pursuing my path: I've always been aware that between her and me the scared one was her. She reminded me of the behaviour of our animals in our yard by the cottage - they show their fangs and claws only when they feel threatened.

She felt an ardent desire to talk openly to him, but a thousand reasons restrained her, first of all the possibility of waking inside him germs of madness by using the wrong words, thereby causing him to fall into the abyss on the edge of which he was poised.

That was the last thing on earth she wanted to provoke - notwithstanding their cool relationship, the age gap between them, their quite different background and past, notwithstanding these reasons and many more, he was terribly dear to her, in a way that mixed compassion with tenderness and gave room also to another, silent feeling that was gliding beneath the surface of her soul, a feeling that Lady Lavinia had spotted even before her, before anybody. Guided by her supernatural knowledge, she had understood everything since the night of the ball, when the naive and inexperienced Page Ashby had wandered in the dark, confused and haggard, and the eyes of her sick husband had followed from the roof the white silhouette of the maiden walking with uncertain pace among the trees. But Page Ashby – now Lady Page – and Lord K, both surveyed by a transcendental force, weren't aware that sometimes immanent, mortal residues remain obstinately stuck to the soul when it leaves this earth, like hard stains on a candid robe that you try to wash off, but can't erase completely.

At this point in the story – after the birds, after the

nightmares, after the daylight hallucination - Lady Page should have understood the lesson quite well. She had. She was equally resolute in being resilient though. And not even the supernatural knowledge of Lavinia was able to detect the inner strength hidden inside the heart of the young lady.

During the following days a heavy melancholy possessed her heart. No other weird events occurred, but her soul was frozen by impotence. No one in the house could satisfy the need for confidence that even a solitary person like her was longing for, as all the personnel were instructed to be discreet and in some cases – like Cezary or even Mrs Haffelaw - had turned openly hostile.

She often went to the stable, passing the time stroking Melmoth's mane and she could detect in his silent big eyes an overwhelming compassion - he had felt the malignity of the birds that time; he had felt the malignity of *her*. He had planted his massive hooves stock still in the ground and had forced Lord K to come back home. Lady Page had never forgotten it. In the same way she was greatly enjoying the company of Ishtar, the well trained dog that had soon got attached to her and the enjoyment, as I said, was mutual - the dog had discovered in Milady the cheerfulness that she had always sought in her master but had never found.

And yet after a while it wasn't enough for Lady Page. The sound of a friendly human word was her utmost need. In her solitude her thoughts began to get magnified.

Soon the thought that maybe she wasn't at all compatible with Lastsight Hill was sneaking into her mind. But then she stood up and thought that it was Lady Lavinia insinuating this kind of perplexities inside her mind, therefore she must not give up. Eventually she started to think that she was becoming demented and often cried silently, overwhelmed.

One day she was leaning by the large mullioned window of the front hall, watching outside. It was early afternoon and Lord K was busy with gardening inside the glasshouse. She was indulging in following his movements - he had rolled his sleeves up and with slow, almost solemn gestures was transposing some berries from small pots to larger ones.

He appeared to my eyes like a will-o'-the-wisp, wreathed in darkness, ready to disappear with the sunshine. An unreal figure, a puppet with invisible strings, guided by an external force from above, because no energy, no lifeblood could come from within. His movements were unnaturally slow, but not slack, as though he was play-acting the role of the officiant in an uncanny ritual, handling the plants with extreme care, sometimes making his thin fingers flow among the leaves and the berries. It was as if his hands had the same, volatile consistence as that of the light leaves and fruits he was touching. Volatile, but not ephemeral - 'poor creature of the earth' I thought, 'you maybe don't want anything else but to reach soon the very earth in which these plants grow their roots.'
In the meantime the broken panel of the glasshouse, still unrepaired after the 'bird incident' and temporarily covered by some wooden boards, stared at me like a big malignant eye, as witness of an episode that I was supposed to keep in my memory forever. Maybe the panel had been left there unrepaired on purpose, because it had to work as a warning to me, to the unwelcome Lady Page. Cezary was working not far away, bent and busy on the shrubs, but I was sure that he was vigilant and with most probability had seen my silhouette at the window. I was ready to see him turn and sneer at me, at any time. My exasperation kept on growing - the faint calmness inside the glasshouse, the big warning eye on its roof, Cezary's malign presence and the unbearable silence inside the

house, where everyone was my enemy...I came to the decision to go out and do something, anything.

It was a warm sunny June afternoon. The door of the glasshouse was flung open, letting in the fresh but pleasant air of the moors. His eyes were following the vivid colours of the raspberries and the bilberries, while he was whispering something to himself.

Amazing how Nature goes on to produce life and vivacity despite the sufferings and the darkness of the human realm.

Suddenly he spotted a slender figure through the leaves and the fruits, standing at the top of the left steps of the house front, the left lateral tongue of Shiva-the-destroyer. It took some time for him to realize that Lady Page was standing there intentionally, staring at him. So far it had never happened that she had addressed him for a particular reason; certainly, he had severely requested never to be bothered and she had scrupulously followed his instructions.

But somehow he had wished that sooner or later she wouldn't.

And now there she was, at the top of the steps, looking firmly at him. Ishtar was standing by her side.

"Look at them. How stupid and selfish on my part to have given way to feelings of jealousy and possessiveness. How marvellous they are, standing there side by side.
They seem to be created on purpose to be fitted for each other.
Not simply the Mistress and her dog. Not the commander and her subordinate. But two peers."

He slowly tried to remove the soil he had on his hands,

keeping his eyes fixed on her profile, then passed through the little door of the glasshouse and went towards her. Apprehension made his heart vacillate a little bit, as if he had been caught by a premonition.

"It's too late to go back on my steps. What shall I say? His eyes…his face…he's approaching. And I feel like I did that evening after the birds - bound to the armchair, incapable of moving, with him staring at me with an indefinite expression that no one would ever be able to interpret…"

"Milady?"
She was still standing at the top of the steps above him, speechless. During all the time he took to climb the stairs she had been staring at him without seeing him.
Finally she found her courage and the words.
"I wonder why we're going on with all this."
"Explain yourself, Milady."
"I mean…you got what you needed, you had my signature on the marriage contract, why do we have to carry on sharing the same roof? Your house and its silence are pleasant to me, but…"
"You need a holiday. You need to leave this place for a while," he cut her short nervously.
"I'm not welcome here, Milord," she nearly shouted. Cezary turned, both surprised and amazed by the unusual scene. Lord K noticed him and his triumphant grimace.
"It's not just him," she went on, tracing his thoughts, "it's…" Something choked her throat. How should she speak explicitly to him about that? Yet she must have lost control of her body language and the sudden turning of her face towards the window of the west wing, followed by a quick irritated gesture of her hand, made everything clear. She saw a flash of understanding in his eyes – exactly as

had happened on the night of the birds when they were by the fire - and she realized that he was slowly coming closer to her. A cold thrill ran through her spine as she saw his face coming just a few inches from hers. Now she could nearly feel his breath…she was sure he was going to shoot questions at her, with a suspicious grim tone, his forehead more frowned than ever.

"I'm going to write to your mother and sister. A summer sojourn at the seaside will be beneficial for all of you, far from these grey skies and inhospitable lands."

He passed her with the same soft-footed pace, almost feline, with which he had climbed the stairs and went quietly inside the house.

She was left stunned, still motionless at the top of the stair. But her body had felt a final indescribable relief and she had started to breathe regularly again.

"She won't come back."

He was leaning on the window frame, exactly the same point from which Lady Page had watched him few days earlier.

"Pardon Milord?" His statement had fallen unexpectedly - we were discussing the current situation of the property and the useless attacks of his father-in-law's lawyer who, after the marriage, had bombarded him with letters.

But it looked as if all that had suddenly turned unimportant to him.

"She won't come back to Lastsight Hill," he repeated. "I am sure that she will return to her family's cottage. How could I blame her?"

I could hardly interpret his countenance, but of one thing I was sure: if, in the place of Lady Page, it had been Miss Deville or one of the Phillips sisters or any of the other rich local ladies, I would have instantaneously interpreted his words as words of triumph. But there was no hint of it in his pitch. It was rather resignation. Wasn't there maybe something else I couldn't trace yet?

"Probably," I answered evasively, pondering over my thoughts. In doing so I slowly neared him and tried to detect something from his features, as he was turned towards the window. I saw the carriage underneath, loaded with a trunk on the back and suddenly I spotted an elegant feminine figure approaching it, dressed in a Bourgogne gown. My eyes turned back to his contrite face and at that precise moment I comprehended what was going on. I instantly lost all my pity for his bereavement and sorrow and started instead to blame his pointless stubbornness, the absolute vanity – yes, vanity – of his grief. He was the masculine version of the grotesque Dickensian character of Miss Havisham, with the difference that he was real before me and, in the place of a decadent wedding table, with a putrefied wedding cake covered with cobwebs and visited by rats, he was keeping a phantom locked in a room of his gloomy mansion. How long could this farce last? Didn't he realize he was rowing against the current of his own vitality? Didn't he realize he was losing his only opportunity to start to live again? I guess a spark of light had been insinuating itself in his heart and mind, but an unwholesome force still vivid inside him, co-opted by a supernatural one outside him, was struggling desperately to render darkness victorious.

I couldn't find the proper words to express all my indignation – a feeling naturally arising out of affection - and stood silent next to him, instead of disclosing my thoughts. How I do regret it! Besides, it was too late. Together we watched the carriage leaving and the pale face of Lady Page bestowing a last glance towards our window, until the coach disappeared among the moors. Ishtar kept on barking at the gate that had been shut by Cezary after the departure and, while somewhere in the west wing someone was silently enjoying the victory, the surrounding gardens looked at once more desolated, almost useless, as if suddenly a grey shroud had been laid on the mansion - I had the very same feeling one has on seeing a hand closing softly the eyelids of a dead friend. After Lady Page's departure, Lastsight Hill appeared to me as a dead creature.'

CHAPTER NINE

GETTING RID OF HER

'Three months later.
September the 3rd 1901.

The thick mist of September chilled the flesh to the bones. Trees had slowly started to drop their leaves and their trunks, darkened by the continuous rain and mist of the season, were starting to divest themselves of their gay garments. The pungent odour of decaying leaves and wet bark turned strangely pleasant. A veil was hovering upon every meadow, cottage and tree, erasing every trace of colour, as though all the hills had simultaneously put a cloak on to face the approaching cold weather.

A dark figure was indulging himself in the fog - a silent, meditating human being, whose presence nobody would have detected if not for the snorting sound of the horse at his side. He was contemplating the profile of his house which stood out on the top of the hill, an imposing goddess victorious against the vapours of the fog.

He had been contemplating the outlines and every corner of his mansion for a considerable time and in the end had found himself reluctant to go back to her - what a strain it had been, to accomplish his own willed seclusion and the preservation of his private grief. He had been desperately seeking a place like that and finally had deliberately chosen Lastsight Hill as his perfect den in which to hide. Now he was starting to perceive that his deliberate choice was turning into a spell cast over him, a trap he had been building with his own hands and from which he could barely escape. He had nothing else to do but accept the course of events as they developed before him.

He stood in front of his house like a damned soul standing in front of his own grave pit, deeply reluctant to accept the fact that his time had arrived and he was lingering on the edge of the grave hoping for something to happen and change the course of things.

But nothing was supposed to happen.

Lady Page had been absent for nearly three months. He hadn't received any letter from her and he had no knowledge about her sojourn. After her departure, no particular event had wakened the regular monotony of his household, which had stubbornly resumed its daily bereavement.

The mist, once a safe, sweet refuge to which he used to entrust his secret tears "as gems in a jewel box", had now turned into a prison. A prison with ephemeral yet cruel bars.

The dark branches of the trees stood gaunt in the air, struggling to find their way through the thick fog, as if they were piercing it in order to extend themselves toward the sky. Dogs' barks and howls were heard from far away fields, prolonging their wails more and more: a poignant chant full of nostalgia, like a last farewell to the cheerfulness of summer.

The chant was so distressing that the horse seemed to be somehow disturbed by it and started to toss his head, his mane shaking wildly in the air. But it wasn't the barking of the dogs, nor their howling that aroused his animal intuition. Something more subtle and not immediately audible was with them in the moors. A presence, a human profile was emerging from the depth of the mist and slowly approaching them.

Lord K felt his heart throbbing loud in his chest. It was a feminine profile. Her head was hooded, her face still indiscernible in the thickness of the haze, but the garment left no room for misgivings: it was undoubtedly the stiff gown of a governess, "his" governess.

"Milady…" he whispered and he almost fainted at the thought that she had finally abandoned her room in the mansion to reach him in the fields. As though she had perceived his hesitations and had come out on purpose to catch him and to drag him back home, back to his grave.

"Let it be what it is," he said to himself as if in a final whisper and lowered his eyes at the approach of the ethereal dark figure floating in the mist.'

At this point of the narrative, MacAllister couldn't help but be vague and provide only a few hints – actually all he knew – about the sojourn of Lady Page by the seaside.

He then went directly to the end of the holiday, when Lady Page…but it's not fair to anticipate here what happened. Before going to that point in the story, we are pleased to say that - as members of the prestigious BSPI - we have been able to reconstruct the most important day of her holiday, thanks to three precious sources: the diary of Lady Page herself, the diary of her dear sister Daphne Ashby and the notes of a foreigner, whose identity will be soon revealed and whose quiet and observing personality, combined with a certain sensibility towards matters going beyond human comprehension, immensely helped us in the business of retracing the following details. We have tried here to provide a reconstruction in line with the narrative reported by Mr MacAllister, in such a way that it will not be disruptive to the story so far disclosed.

This is exactly what happened just a few days before Lord K had been surprised by the sudden apparition of the woman in dark among the hills...

REPORT OF LADY PAGE'S SOJOURN ON THE YORKSHIRE COAST
August 30th 1901.

Cheerful were the faces, the ladies' cheeks slightly blushing upon the last sunshine of the season and the gaiety of the moment, the smiling men holding their white hats and wafting them like fans. The sea was roaring harmlessly beneath the cliff and the seagulls were flying noisily over them, as if they wanted to join the party.

The sky was incredibly clear and no cottage nor any building was visible in a two mile radius, with the exception of the old castle, whose ruins were mesmerizing.

They had spread on the grass a cloth for the food and some blankets to sit on.

Everybody was happy and cheerful. Everybody, but one.

We imagine that every one of you has, at least once, experienced being in a situation that has got all the conditions to be pleasant or even happy, but that doesn't fit at all your own inward feelings of the moment and in which - regardless of all the good premises - you feel the utmost distress and wish with your whole being to be somewhere else, maybe in a solitary place where nobody will ask you questions.

That was the case for Lady Page during the beautiful and sunny afternoon of August by the cliffs on the north-eastern coast of England - the sun's rays seemed to refuse to kiss her skin; the sea, which she couldn't admire, arrived with a threatening noise at her ears, not to mention the annoying seagulls above her, which were sadly recalling the appalling episode of the crows flying in circles above the glasshouse.

But most of all, it was the human party surrounding her which was particularly irritating.

Apart from her mother, Daphne and Donovan the party was thus composed: Mr and Mrs Wateley, a kind couple who lived in the neighbourhood; Mrs Loretta Monti, a middle aged widow with Italian origins, a friend of the couple above and lastly the Phillips sisters along with the hateful Mr Walsh and Young Phillips.

The latter was the really upsetting surprise for Lady Page, who had never thought for a moment about the eventuality of meeting again her vain suitor, together with his arrogant brother-in-law.

His sisters, once the first to mock the Ashbys, had suddenly turned into their best friends. But if this could work well with Mary Ann and Daphne, who didn't have a clue about the self-conceit that once animated the young ladies, it wasn't quite the same for Lady Page, who quietly avoided any attempt at conversation and could scarcely hide her own disdain towards them.

The detail couldn't escape Eugene Phillips, who was observing the scene in amusement and in a growing rapture of admiration toward the woman whom he had never ceased to be fond of.

But her countenance didn't escape Daphne either, who was getting more and more worried about her sister. She was puzzled by Page's frowning eyes and silence, which were in sharp contrast to the joyful party gathered by the sea. To tell the truth, she had been worried about her sister all through the summer, but for a number of reasons she had never addressed the issue either with Page or with her mother.

Regarding Mr. Walsh, the contempt was mutual – Page had never forgotten his remark about women and literature - and that was good enough to keep him far from any attempt at conversation.

'Darling, the Cotgraves' cottage shouldn't be far from here, should it?' Mrs Wateley asked her husband. He was standing on the brink of the cliff, admiring the sea, while she was sipping her tea on the grass.

'Well, it should be four or five miles from here,' he said, turning around with his binoculars in his hands, 'but I might be wrong - let's say I was a little bit confused that night,' he added, frowning behind the glasses.

'What was the matter?' Young Phillips asked, chuckling. 'Were you exaggerating about your drink, Mr Wateley?'

'Oh no, nothing of the sort, I'm not that type. It was just…never mind. It's…'

'…Hilarious,' his wife intervened.

'How can you really define it hilarious, sweetheart?' he replied, half embarrassed and half amused. 'Perhaps for you, it was a source of entertainment, yet not for me. I dare say it was an eerie experience indeed, I don't think I could ever go through it again.'

'You make us curious, Mr. Wateley, now you have to tell us about it'. It was Mary Ann speaking, whose pleasure of being mingled with "the high ranked society" - as she used to call it - had made her a daring talker.

'Oh, it's just nonsense.' Mr Wateley kept hold of his binoculars, pretending to follow the idle route of the seagulls, but his wife's smile revealed that they were going to disclose something intriguing.

'It was a séance,' she said abruptly, to general amazement. 'Allegedly, Mrs Cotgrave has 'the Gift''. She ably paused for a moment, looking attentively at the listening audience around her and, weighing on purpose each word, she said solemnly, 'She can see the dead and talk with them.'

She was undoubtedly a skilful teller. She had another sip of her tea and then added jauntily, changing the tone of her voice, 'Well, I can't actually say with certainty whether it was staged or not, I may only say it was an unusual experience.'

She smiled, giving a glance towards her husband, who had remained still where he was, his shoulders turned to her and to the others.

'Well, it seems that nowadays some people like to indulge in oddities like that,' young Phillips said while his eyes were seeking Lady Page's. 'Maybe to them the dead turn out to be more entertaining than the living.'

Lady Page hadn't got the hint at first. But she gradually began to understand what he wanted to drive at. At the same time, she realized the unprecedented feeling of being hurt by a reference to Lord K. Her mouth couldn't stay shut. She was no longer at his family's dependence, she had no obligation to bite her tongue and little she cared about how inconvenient it could be in the presence of her mother and sister. She could speak for herself now, every responsibility was hers.

'To be fair, it looks like séances and other kinds of 'oddities', as you call them, are not a mere prerogative of a few eccentric individuals, but are indeed common among the so called 'good society'. They are quite in fashion, I dare say.' She spoke with a hint of defiance that didn't escape Daphne.

'I took part at one of those events too,' Mrs Monti said laconically, in a low voice. Her comment arrived unexpectedly and brought a weight of silence to the middle of the animated conversation. She added nothing else and everybody was staring at her in expectation, when she hastily added, almost apologetically, 'it was a long time ago, in a small village in southern Italy. I was a very young and impressionable lady.'

'My dear Mr Phillips, I assure you that Mrs Cotgrave is a very respectable lady, not devoted at all to 'oddities' in her everyday life,' Mrs Wateley finally said, breaking the weird curtain of embarrassment that had wrapped the party during the last exchanges. Mr Phillips bowed his head to apologize. 'On that occasion,' she added, 'it was just at our friend's insistence, whose child had died prematurely, that she agreed to perform a séance.'

'And what happened then? Can you tell us?' Mary Ann asked boldly.

'Well, after a while she rolled her eyes and said that she had a message from the deceased child for his mother. She said...'

'Enough.' Lady Page got up and, under the astonished eyes of her sister, made her way towards the cliff's edge, beside Mr Wateley, while his wife was finishing her grotesque story. Donovan, who had been listening to the story of the séance with eager attention, suddenly got up at the sight of his sister leaving and reached her side.

'Why don't we all go and pay a visit to this lady?' Young Phillips's voice echoed loudly, reaching her ears. 'You said she lives few miles away from here.'

'I don't think we can pop in to the Cotgraves' house without giving any notice,' Mr Wateley said from the cliff. 'Oh, don't be silly, my darling, you know they're not as formal as that. I am sure they will be glad to see us,' Mrs Wateley said. 'On the contrary, I think it a great idea. What a perfect ending to a lovely afternoon!' she added, getting up.

And that's how they finally dismissed their doubts, by agreeing to a collective expedition whose real purpose was to exorcise their fear of the unknown through laughter and debunking.

It is almost superfluous to note that, according to our experience as investigators, such a response is quite typical among people whose attitude towards life relies almost exclusively on rationalism and common sense.

It was five o'clock and upon their arrival the sight of the cottage appeared amidst the moors as a welcoming friend, its roof sparkling in the glory of the afternoon, the flowers of the front garden waving gaily at them and the ivy creeping happily all around it, neatly cut by window and door frames.

Mr Walsh, Young Phillips and the sisters arrived first, riding in the brand new car that Walsh had purchased just few weeks earlier and that – needless to say – he was driving with visible pride. After a while, the two carriages with the rest of the party reached the vehicle. The car's cold metal frame was shining in the setting sun, in stark contrast with the shiny but warm manes of the horses, while they were still shaking their heads and the steam was billowing from their nostrils.

The Cotgraves displayed all the sincere warmth and cordiality that one would expect from a host. Nothing suggested any idea of dark rooms, heavy curtains and eerie whispers.

All the party felt immediately at ease in the cosy home of the Cotgraves and the references made to supernatural practices appeared suddenly distant and unreal in everyone's mind. They were dismissed as mere bizarre insinuations, results of a lazy afternoon by the seaside.

Mrs Cotgrave was a kind old lady. Numerous wrinkles were embroidering her pale face, especially around her eyes. Over time, her memory had suffered considerable loss and, as her husband – a witty gentleman whose hair was as white as snow – echoed all the things she said, the result was rather hilarious.

'We used to go every day to the cliff when we were young, or further, to the seaside over there. We loved to have long walks with Mr and Mrs Jones and sometimes we used to stop by the sea. We would spread the cloth on the ground, have a sandwich and enjoy the breeze - that was all we could have asked.'

'Oh yes dear, we did enjoy long walks very much. We didn't have a picnic only, though, we used to play chess as well, unless it was too windy for that. The wind would have upset everything and raised sand from the seaside.'

'Which seaside?'

'The seaside you have just mentioned, my dear.'

'I have never mentioned a seaside, darling. As I was saying…'

Chuckles would follow their exchanges, but they seemed not to be bothered by them. Lady Page felt annoyed by all that. Her mind was elsewhere and the last thing she cared about was listening to the nostalgic memories of a forgetful old couple.

Feeling bad about it and wishing to avoid any awkwardness, she asked permission to have a walk in their rear garden, on the excuse of a sudden migraine and the need of some fresh air. Once outside and once she shut the glass door that from the sitting room gave directly onto the garden, she felt immediately relieved. Now she had the opportunity of finally being alone for a while. It was only her, the plants and the moors, whose wind had started to blow over the low brick wall which enclosed the Cotgraves' property. Whenever she turned, she could spot the faces of Young Phillips and Mr Walsh, both red in the attempt to control their chuckles, or the two sisters exchanging glances behind their fans. Only Mrs Loretta Monti – *'a thoughtful, generally reserved woman'*, as she pointed out in her diary – wasn't cheerful. It seemed that she was staring in perplexity at the young lady in the garden, regardless of the others around her. To Lady Page's relief, their voices couldn't be heard, covered as they were by the whistling of the wind - getting stronger and stronger with the approaching of the dusk - and by the noise of the sea, despite its distance from the spot. Its smell, aided by the powerful gusts, was intoxicating her.

Standing alone there, in the garden of foreign people, on the north-eastern coast of England and away from her own environment, she started a very honest conversation with herself.

You have run away from Lastsight Hill looking for someone to talk to, begging a piece of empathy from a human heart and now you find repulsive the very same humanity you were craving, your own family included. What do you want, then, Page? What's the source of both your restlessness and melancholy? Ah, I have the feeling that among the bushes of these moors I will soon perceive the stout profile of Melmoth's head and the gaunt figure of his master by his side. But it won't happen. They're miles away, enwrapped by their bereavement. How pathetic they sometimes look! Yet, I'm so cruel to think in this way…and I can't help thinking about this man and his faithful horse. Melmoth, the guardian of his tears. The one who is in charge of looking after his soul. The one who doesn't allow his master to take perilous paths. I can't rest without this vision of the two, their bond is so tender and reassuring at the same time. I miss them. I miss them tremendously. I miss Lastsight Hill, I miss Ishtar. Where should I go? Which is my home now? My home is where my heart and soul drive me. And my heart and soul drive me back to Lastsight Hill.

The sky was changing colours quite rapidly, rolling towards the ambiguous vagueness of twilight and the wind was growing more and more ferocious, as though it was biting up furiously the setting sun. She glanced beyond the brick wall at the moors around, where the wild bushes and the heathers were bent mercilessly under the blasts. She sat down by the wooden bench set graciously by a corner of the garden, among anemones and rhododendrons, when once again she felt the disquieting sensation that she had experienced inside the glasshouse - the little, neat garden of the Cotgraves was working as an *hortus conclusus* – an enclosed space - trying to protect her as best it could. Protect her from the vast moors, which seemed to menace that infinitesimal, ridiculous, man-made square of greenery; protect her from the sea, which had started to roar madly underneath the very cliff where they had just spent their lovely afternoon.

Then she finally roused herself, turned towards the house and…she couldn't believe her eyes.

Mrs Cotgrave, the witty Mrs Cotgrave, the very same woman who had been lively entertaining her guests a few minutes earlier, was staring distressedly at her from behind the window, apparently shouting something, struggling because of the grip of Mrs Monti on one side and of Young

Phillips on the other, while Mary Ann, Daphne and the others stood as if paralyzed in consternation. The old woman's hairstyle was completely spoiled during the struggle and locks of grey hair fell loose before her eyes. Her face was utterly disfigured, a mask of terror and anguish.

Eventually, she had the force to release herself from the grip of her guests and reached the handle of the door.

'Get rid of her!' were the first words she uttered.

'Get rid of her!' she repeated vigorously, and she went on and on with the same formula, tirelessly.

'Get rid of her!' she repeated again, this time getting closer and pointing her finger to the poor Lady Page, who could do nothing other than recoil, confused and frightened by the transfigured woman.

The suitcases lay open on the bed, empty.

She stood as if hypnotised by the wide open wardrobe, her eyes fixed on the dark gown she had used as a governess and which her instinct had suggested she should carry with her even on holiday.

'That's what I am,' she thought. And so she put it on.

A knock on the door. Daphne.

She came in silently, looking perplexed at her sister's preparations and at her attire.

'You're taking that woman's words too personally,' she dared to say in a very low voice.

Lady Page was caught by surprise. During the two days following the 'incident' at the Cotgraves nobody had ever even hinted at what had happened. It had been immediately cancelled by their subconscious as being too disturbing.

In reality, its mark hadn't gone away at all and the memory of that event, fresh as it was, floated above them uncontrolled.

Only Mrs Loretta Monti had tried in vain to approach Milady about the above episode, saying that she had 'something important' to tell her about it. But Lady Page was so upset that she didn't want to hear a word and had retired to her room since the night they had come back home, claiming that she didn't want to see anybody. A fact that she deeply regretted later on.

'Mrs Cotgrave is right,' she pointed out, 'you'd better get rid of me. It is clear that I am not welcome among this party.'

'Page, please don't say that.'

'Don't try to stop me, Daphne. Besides, that is what I feel. I must go. I don't belong here.'

'Where do you belong, then?'

She didn't answer. But started to smile in return and to caress the stiff and coarse material of her gown. It was so solid to her touch, which made her feel comfortable and self-confident, compared to the airy, impalpable laces and silks of her lady-like summer gowns. She felt a tremendous power in herself and a consolidated yearning to go back to her mansion, Lastsight Hill.

'Page, I've got something to tell you.'

She was abruptly brought back to the petty reality of life by her sister.

'I know maybe it's not the proper moment for this, but I can't help it, I want to share it with you. Young Phillips proposed to me,' and in saying so she couldn't stifle a smile.

In a few seconds I had to decide. Telling her the truth, putting her on guard about the falsity of the man - but this would have been a blow to her own sensibility and artlessness - or saying nothing at all. In the end, I didn't want to break her unconditional trust in the good faith of other fellow human beings.

'He's so charming and good mannered. Mother would be delighted, wouldn't she?'
'Yes, Daphne. I am sure she would.'

She was so happy, how could I destroy such happiness? Sometimes telling lies is not a sin at all. Truth can be brutal and harmful. I had no right to pollute her pure soul with the fumes of my disillusion. I am glad I supported the plan of my beloved sister to marry a man I deeply hate. I would do it again.

She hugged her sister warmly.
'May you be happy.'

That evening, during the journey back to Lastsight Hill, lulled by the fast driving coach, her eyes stuck on the moors outside the window, she recalled all the feelings she had felt and the eldritch events that had happened during her past stay in Lastsight Hill. The attack attempted by the birds, the frightening vision she had of Lady Lavinia's portrait, her appalling nightmares and the constant aversion of Lord K's valet Cezary. Everything sounded like a clear warning to stay away from that mansion. Any reasonable young lady in her same situation would have been content to do so. She was rushing instead right into the lion's jaws. Why?
Suddenly her mind was crossed by a flashing thought, sparkling with all the clarity of certainty. Mrs Cotgrave had clearly involved her in her violent edict, but Page was not the *object* of it. Lady Page was the one who had to do the ridding, not the one to be got rid of. Bearing this in mind,

she prepared her spirit to face a turning point in the household of Lastsight Hill.

CHAPTER TEN

HEART AND SOUL

'E tu che se' costì, anima viva,

pàrtiti da cotesti che son morti.'

'And thou who art here, living soul,

Depart from these who are dead.'[4]

Dante Alighieri, *Inferno* III 82-84

'Do you remember where we were last time? I was telling you about the morning when, during one of his usual walks with Melmoth on the hills, Lord K perceived a human

---

[4] Translation by Leni Remedios.

figure among the mist.'

'One moment,' Peter interrupted him, 'all this happened during Lady Page's absence, didn't it?'

'Quite correct,' replied MacAllister, 'and here everything matches.' He took a puff of smoke from his inseparable pipe.

'"Let it be what it is," were his last words when we interrupted the story. And in his deranged mind he thought that his time had really come and Lavinia had come out of her room to drive him to the land of the dead, to which she belonged - a feminine version of Charon, gliding on the thick hazy streams. The misty hills, pierced here and there by the gaunt branches, provided the panorama that fitted extraordinarily well his distressed frame of mind: a landscape at the same time mystical and hellish...'

'Erm...,' Mr Toulson cleared his throat, 'Charon?'

'Oh, sure,' said Mr MacAllister apologetically, startled as if awakening from a dream. 'According to the fascinating Greek mythology,' he explained as soon as he recomposed himself, 'Charon was the boatman who carried the souls of the dead from the world of the living to the underworld. The two worlds were imagined as separated by a river. Centuries later, Dante described him in his *Divine Comedy*, during his fictional journey there. This is how the dark figure who was walking through the mist appeared to Lord K. Then, something apparently trivial but indeed utterly shocking struck him. It was a hint of colour, precisely a drop of red. It looked out of place in the black and grey landscape all around him. He didn't know what to make of it. It even made him feel strangely uncomfortable. It was nothing other than a lock of hair, popping out the hood of the figure who was now at few yards from his person. An unprecedented feeling crept into him, immediately fighting with the mournful peace he had prepared for himself.

Reluctantly, despite his own will, he felt reanimated, like a Golem in which a breath of life has been instilled, as if a subterranean stream was dragging him back to the realm of the living. Eventually, this powerful force led him to stretch his hands forth and there they met other hands, not at all the cold and ephemeral hands of an undead, but vibrant and warm ones. He dared to murmur, as if reciting a liberating prayer: "Lady Page…"

"What do you mean with 'Milady is not in her room?" Mrs Haffelaw's tone made the young maid panic more than she already was.

"I swear, I got in her room at the usual time in the morning, and she wasn't there! I then checked everywhere else in the house," Joanna replied in tears.

"Have you checked in the library? You know that Milady's habits are not…ordinary," she commented, lowering her voice while saying the last word and looking around.

"Yes, I have checked even there," the maid replied sobbing. "Has anything bad happened to her? Milord looks so strange sometimes…"

"Very well, please compose yourself first," Mrs Haffelaw interrupted, this time calmly, grabbing her by her shoulders. "Now, I will summon Cezary and Neal and will ask them about it. She must have gone to the gardens. You'd better go and wash your face. Then carry on tidying up the other rooms. A sobbing maid is no use to anybody."

You can only imagine how surprising it was for Mrs Haffelaw when, a couple of hours later, she saw from the window Lord K and Lady Page walking back home side by side.

After a nourishing meal, the two met in the drawing room. I remember, I was waiting in the antechamber for our weekly meeting. We needed to discuss reports and general issues concerning his estate. I will never forget the puzzled and grieved air Milady had when she left the room and her eyes met mine. How naïve on my part to ascribe it to her tiredness. If I only had followed my intuition, I could have done something to prevent the grave episode I'm going soon to describe you. But first let's go back to the exchange my Master and Milady had in the drawing room.

"I have to apologize for the things I said to you before leaving," she said softly, resting her hands on the arm of the sofa and leaning her head on them gently. She looked at the sky out of the window. "I have fully realized I belong in some way to Lastsight Hill. I have missed this place".

He sat down beside her, slowly bent towards her and softly touched her hair. She closed her eyes and went on, "I can't understand how my dear sister is looking for the company of those people," she sighed, "and asking for their approval. She's so tender and artless. She is not able to see..."

"Not able to see what?" he whispered gently, foreseeing the answer.

"I'd like to be like her sometimes," she went on, regardless of his question. "I'd like not to see, not to understand, gliding on the surface of life, incapable of seeing through. I've been taught that cleverness and acumen are good qualities, I've been encouraged to develop these gifts, through learning and studying. And then I found myself vulnerable, unsafe, tottering among the unveiled truths while everyone around me seems not to see them. Isn't it that ignorance keeps people safe and happy? A plain, sweet, calm kind of happiness. No alarms, no wildness, no doubts. Like the smooth surface of the sea when no wind bewilders it. Isn't it?"

Her eyes glared. He was touched to his deepest by her words. And yet, something was perturbing the scene.

"That's why I belong here."

He slowly turned his head and glanced over his shoulder, keeping close to her, instinctively, as if in the act of protecting her.

"That's why I've missed this place…and you…"

He pressed her shoulder with his hand and grew alarmed.

"Here I feel free, here I don't have to pretend to be someone different from what I am."

He seized her shoulder even more, with trembling hands. She kept her eyes closed. She could feel his breath growing faster and faster, in unison with the throb of her own heart.

"Maybe we can share our lives in some way."

He looked behind and started.

"Maybe we can be good companions and…"

"Promise me you will be with Mrs Haffelaw during the time I will be busy with MacAllister," he said abruptly. She opened her eyes, struck by his sudden change of tone and subject.

"Milord…"

"Promise me you will not stay alone!" A hint of irritation was in his voice.

She then turned completely and stared at him, puzzled. He immediately looked behind, as if to verify there was someone there. But nobody was there. His face was pale and grim.

She nodded quietly, stood up and slowly walked backwards towards the door, staring at him.

"I promise."

I finally got in.

"Is Milady ill?" I asked softly. "Maybe the long journey was too tiring for her, was it?'

"I suppose it was," he answered evasively.

But nothing could escape me and I immediately realized that there was something wrong. With my usual practical manners, I laid the papers on the table and started to talk about possessions, harvests and so on, absolutely aware that he was not listening, but sure that somehow I could gradually drive my master's attention to other subjects, rather than those he was indulging in. Only I and no one else had the ability to do this - bringing him from his own world back to reality. Indeed, after a while he was talking with me about peasants, stock and fees to pay.

While we were so engaged, Lady Page was sitting in a little room not far from us, with Mrs Haffelaw.

"Promise me you will not stay alone!"

The latter was knitting, the noise of the needles being the only sound piercing the silence. Lady Page was staring at the fire, still puzzled by what had just happened in the drawing room.

What did his words mean?

"Was your vacation pleasant, Milady?"

"It was, thank you."

"I am glad of it."

In the light of what she had experienced in the past, it wasn't so difficult to sense what his odd behaviour could be ascribed to, and yet…

"You seem to be still tired? Shall I prepare another bath for you later?"

"Later will be fine. I will first wait for Milord to finish his business with Mr MacAllister."

"As Milady wishes."

…it was plausible that the mix of emotions he was going through was exaggerating any sensation that crossed his mind, perceiving threats even in the most harmless situations.

Lady Page looked around her - there was nothing to do and the formal conversation with Mrs Haffelaw was annoying her. She didn't want to talk at all. She just wanted to be alone and think about what had just happened. Alone. But she couldn't stay alone. She had promised.

Suddenly she had an idea and got up.

"I will take a book from the library and be back in a minute."

Mrs Haffelaw nodded politely but at the same time scrutinizing Milady, unobserved. Lady Page didn't need to justify herself; she wasn't obliged to give company to a humble housekeeper. Of course, Mrs Haffelaw knew nothing about the promise. However, she wasn't unwary. Since their employers had come back from the moors, neither of them had bothered to provide any explanation about the sudden disappearance of Milady, which had made Joanna lose her nerve and made her worry, despite her external composure. Not that they had to. Yet, after years of housekeeping under different families, she was able to sense a perturbance in a household only by a slight change in the facial expression of her employers. Her intuition, summed with the memory of the past events, suggested that something was going on. But, in the end, it was none of her business. She wasn't supposed to meddle with their problems, real or imaginary.

Lady Page closed the door quietly behind her. She passed along the drawing room and attempted to eavesdrop - Lord K and I were involved in an animated discussion. Meanwhile in the main hall the maids were brushing the carpets. From the outside the voices of Cezary and Neal were heard, busy with their gardening: everything was in its right place. Everything was following the ordinary daily course. She moved straight towards the library, pacified and self-confident. She went in.

Lavinia had been hovering above the pair, looking at them, with her pale face and her dark, plain frock, while they were talking in the drawing room. She had appeared like a hungry vulture perched on a tree branch, staring at its prey with eager eyes. With a thrill of horror, Lord K realised that it was definitely the very first time she had left her own room since they had moved to Lastsight Hill. She had never previously dared to do so. That room was a sort of sanctuary specifically devoted to a strange sort of goddess. There were her belongings and her portrait; there they met every single evening after dinner. But she had never gone out. Even when he started to go there less frequently. It was a kind of silent agreement between them. And besides, gods usually don't go out of their sanctuary. He experienced then a disquieting feeling stealing across his heart, a dreadful premonition. For the first time he started to feel genuine fear.

There was a dead silence inside the library. And it was freezing - the fire hadn't been lit. The weak light of the dusk was still entering by the large windows that faced onto the front lawns. Soon it would be fading away.

The top of the glasshouse was visible from where she was standing and the cracked panel, still unrepaired and roughly covered by scrubby old wooden boards, vexed her sight and gave her a dismal feeling.

She started to pace among the tall shelves. She had no idea about the book she meant to read - her mind was too busy for reading and she was simply looking for a pretext not to chat with Mrs Haffelaw. Eventually the choice fell on a little volume in the poetry section, a collection of Coleridge poems, and when she attempted to reach it, she was suddenly struck on her neck by something hard, and fainted senseless on the floor.

"Where is Milady?"
The unhinged tone of Milord startled an astonished Mrs Haffelaw.
"She went to take a book in the library and then..."
"When did it happen?" he urged.
"Well, she said she would be back in a minute but…"
"Well?"
"I suppose about fifteen minutes have passed and she's not back yet."
He sprang out of the room immediately.
The poor Mrs Haffelaw tried in vain to chase him, "For God's sake, what is the matter, Milord?" But he wouldn't hear anything, he just climbed the stairs with all the speed of which he was capable. Panting heavily, I followed him till I found him standing by the wide open library door and the scene that presented itself beyond his tall dark figure was something I had never expected to see - the towering shelves were completely empty, like rows of ghastly giants deprived of their souls. On the floor lay mountains of books, scattered everywhere, most of them open. Some pages had been torn away in the collapse and the air shift due to the door being flung open made them float around. "Jesus Christ," I couldn't help exclaiming. And at the same time, approaching my master, I could see his face pale as ever, paralyzed by horror. His bulging eyes were apparently trying to detect anything – the fingers of a hand, a lock of hair, the fringe of a gown – emerging somewhere, but the scene was so utterly chaotic that eyes struggled to spot any outline. He didn't move at all until, with a sudden and firm motion, he sprang forward to a point quite near the windows where, among scattered books with blood-

stained edges, the scene was dominated by an open volume. Its illustrations and poems were facing the ceiling: Coleridge's *Cristabel*. With resolute and precise gestures – the tremors of his limbs had suddenly ceased, giving way to a steadiness of movement - he threw the volumes away, one after the other, until eventually the body of Lady Page emerged, face downwards on the floor. He turned her. She was lying senseless.

The blow on her neck had made her faint and lose consciousness. The first thing she had seen on awakening had been a gap in the row of books standing on the shelf behind her. With a great effort, feeling dizzy, she gradually managed to sit up on the floor and see what had actually hit her: *The Seeress of Prevorst*, an essay about the sensitive Friederike Hauffe. She chuckled at the thought that, in a house haunted by a phantom, a book about a woman who used to talk with the dead had done harm to her. But her good spirit was soon interrupted by a rattle coming from the other aisle. With a further, extreme effort, grasping at the closest shelf, she stood up, reached the bottom of the aisle in which she was situated and eventually turned the corner. What she saw went beyond anything she had ever thought she would witness in Lastsight Hill - a copy of the *Arabian Nights* was floating in the air, wide open, spinning slowly. She gaped incredulous, mesmerized by the revolving wonder. Soon after, a copy of Dante's *Inferno* departed quietly from its place, following a linear, horizontal route, till approached her person, opened and started to flutter its pages allowing her to enjoy the stupendous illustrations by Gustav Doré.

Thus Spoke Zarathustra, *The Time Machine*, *The Last Man*: an army of paper creatures abandoned their quiet dens, one after the other, and took on independent life, displaying their lines and pictures in front of her as if in a parade. A sweet rapture took possession of her and she couldn't help but walk among them - now they were surrounding her like vibrant entities celebrating the most delightful of the Sabbaths, in an enchantment she wished could never end. So utterly charmed she was that she tried to reach them, in vain. They seemed as though they wanted to be chased, as though they were taking part in a game and she was fully, blindly enjoying it, like the old times at the cottage, when she would chase her siblings in the garden, in total freedom of mind.

In her delight she hadn't noticed that the books had gained speed. Gradually, they had started not only to rotate on themselves, but also to revolve along invisible orbits and at every single revolution they grew faster...and faster...till a sheet, a single innocuous sheet, hurt her face sharply.

"Oh!" she awoke from the stupor she had hitherto been immersed in. More than the physical pain, it had been the awakening from the enchantment that had shocked her. The papery creatures around her appeared now in all their appalling truth: no longer cheerful companions in a game, but maddened pawns moved by a steady, evil hand whose evident intention was purposely to harm her.

They were revolving at an uncontrolled speed and she desperately realized that she was in danger and that at this point there was no way to escape. She attempted to cling to the nearest shelf but another sharp blow arrived first at her face and then at her left hand. The creatures, a sample of the best masterpieces ever produced by the human mind, began a real escalation of terror against the poor Lady Page, lacerating her exposed limbs, with which she was trying to protect her head. Finally they threw themselves with the utmost violence against her frail body, among them volumes of considerable weight and size,

173

which afflicted her with the fury of the worst demons.
The shelves around her were almost completely emptied.
Entirely covered by a heap of books, she could feel her
senses and her consciousness abandoning her, while she
could still feel the very last strokes of the few volumes left.'

CHAPTER ELEVEN

HEAVEN AND HELL

'Miles away a lady was looking out of a window by the Yorkshire coast. The sky had been grey and sullen for the last few days and the sea looked enraged by an obstinate, unceasing wind.

"I don't like it," she thought with a sigh.

She felt deeply concerned and the unexplainable, strong sense of foreboding she had had three days earlier came violently back. The wild nature outside seemed an appalling omen mirroring her feelings.

But her external countenance was composed and dignified. As a matter of fact, throughout her life she had never had reason to lose control of her feelings, despite all stereotypes about the passionate Italian temper.

"Mrs Monti," the querulous voice of Mary Ann Kavanagh Ashby interrupted her chain of thought, "we were told you wished to have a word with us soon after breakfast." She had stepped into the room with her daughter Daphne by

175

her side, but a third party was lingering at the threshold.

"Do you mind Young Phillips joining us?"

"Of course I don't."

He hinted a little bow and closed the door behind him. They all took a seat by the fire.

"So, what do you mean to tell us about? I confess I am a little bit alarmed and..."

"Yes, you'd better be alarmed, Madam, I am sorry to say." Mary Ann was shocked by her words and stared speechless at the Italian lady.

"Would you...would you be so kind as to give us some more explanation, please?" she staggered eventually. She and Daphne were now sitting on the very edge of the sofa, their heads getting closer to one another, their eyes fixed on Mrs Monti's face. Meanwhile, Young Phillips sat quietly on the nearby armchair, idly smoking his pipe, quite regretting having joined them. He was looking away, distracted. He didn't like that foreign woman. The feeling was mutual and had started since the night at the Cotgrave's.

"Well," Loretta Monti cleared her throat with a cough and began, "I have reasons to believe that your daughter and sister, Lady Page, is in danger."

Young Phillips turned his attention to the lady with a quick movement of his eyes.

"Could you please tell us," Daphne dared to ask, cautiously, "could you tell us upon what basis you assert this?"

"I know it might sound ridiculous. You have the right to feel incredulous about it and to dismiss what I am about to say but... I'm not able to give you much further explanation. I had bad dreams and I strongly sense that..."

"Mrs Monti, aren't you following the same nonsense as Mrs Cotgrave?" Mary Anne interrupted her, irritated.

"Please, mother, let her finish." Daphne grabbed her arm. Young Phillips scoffed impatiently, shaking his head.

"What kind of dreams, Mrs Monti? Please carry on."

"I dare tell you this because I had a similar experience in the past, years ago in my country. I wasn't believed at the time, everybody around treated me with disdain or even mocked me. Later on, my foreboding turned out to be tragically correct."

She half smiled at the thought. Then her face became suddenly sad. "In my dream Lady Page was alone, I suppose somewhere in the countryside, and she had been hurt - her face and her whole body were wounded. When I awoke, I couldn't remember who or what inflicted this on her, though."

She shook her head as if trying to recollect her memories.

"And this is not all - after the afternoon by the seaside and the visit to the Cotgraves, I had some strange feelings of premonition, Mrs Ashby." She lifted her chin and looked elsewhere, absorbed. "There is something wrong over there," she added.

"Do you mean Lastsight Hill?" asked Daphne.

She simply nodded with a sigh.

"What premonitions did you have? Please, for God's sake, be more precise Mrs Monti!" Mary Ann implored, struggling between incredulity and genuine concern.

"I already told you, it's nothing well-defined, it is just a strong feeling that has been accompanying me for days. But on one point I am sure -" she added firmly, "what Mrs Cotgrave told her that day was true - '*Get rid of her*' she said, didn't she?" she carried on, this time looking straight into Mary Anne's eyes, "yet, did not refer to..."

Young Phillips now burst into laughter, catching everybody by surprise.

"If I were you, I would not dare laugh, Mr Phillips," Mrs

Monti remarked, maintaining her usual composure.

This irritated Young Phillips even further.

"I'll tell you what it is," he started in a nervous tone while standing up and beginning to pace up and down. "Mrs Ashby is right in referring to it as nonsense."

"Mr Phillips, I beg you..." Daphne tried to stop him in vain.

"Yes, it might be that Lady Page is in danger, but surely not because of any of the supernatural elements you sense and about which you haven't a clue, as seems to be evident." He had raised the tone of his voice, and his face had reddened. "The danger is actually much more grounded on earth and lies in her mad husband, towards whom she seems to have developed an insane tenderness."

"Mr Phillips, please, how dare you to talk in this way about my child!"

This time Mary Anne intervened.

"Mrs Ashby, I frankly can't believe that smart women like you and your elder daughter are relying on the words of a visionary," he went on regardless. "We are talking about a man, Lord K, who lives in eternal bereavement, a man who disdains any human being and prefers to dwell in the memory of his dead wife."

"His wife...," murmured Mrs Monti while looking away. But Young Phillips didn't notice, caught up as he was in his rant.

"No wonder she is in danger, staying next to a man who despises the entire human race," he continued. "I guess that it is true what has been rumoured, that he brought the corpse of his wife with him and buried it somewhere in the manor's gardens."

"In the greenhouse, to be precise," Daphne added whispering.

"Daphne, don't tell me you're paying attention to the silly stories of your brother," Mary Ann cut in.

"Madam," the calm voice of Mrs Monti brought them back to order, "I suggest you reach Milady as soon as possible. Leave today, don't waste any time," she added.

At that moment the door swung open and Mr Walsh came in. "What is going on here? I heard your voice from the other side of the building, Phillips."

"Mother, I will call for a coach and leave this afternoon," said Daphne suddenly.

"I am coming with you."

Their scepticism seemed to have left them at once.

"Please, mother, leave it to me. You will stay here with Donovan - a journey like that can be extremely tiring for you. Besides, you are in distress."

"Wait a minute," Young Phillips interrupted, "Walsh, maybe you can take us back to the village, can you? By car, it will take far less time than by coach and horses."

Daphne looked incredulously at him.

"Of course I can, but what is this all about?"

They left that very same morning.

Several hours earlier, Lady Page had been lying in her bed in Lastsight Hill, wrapped in a sort of bitter-sweet stupor, her wounded body aching from the thuds of the books, her mind wandering through what had happened the previous night after the hideous incident in the library. She turned her head towards the empty space beside her.

Going back...going back in her mind...indulging...

He had applied some sort of plant-based ointment to her injuries. In order to do so, she had had to expose large portions of her body and it had all awakened a mix of new feelings in her, beside the embarrassment of constantly having the omnipresent Mrs Haffelaw in the room. Then, he had recommended deep rest and bidden the housekeeper to provide a jar of water and some food by the bedside table. Lastly, he had asked for a maid to sit just outside the room, at disposal for any kind of request.

But then it was impossible for her to sleep. How could she? Both pleasant and disquieting thoughts were intersecting in her memory. While her body could scarcely move without pain, her mind was wandering restlessly, going back to the misty hills where they had met the day before, but particularly to the library, over and over again, the memory of the books whirling around still vivid, the claustrophobic sensation of being buried under a heap of books still choking her throat.

Tired of lying on her back, with some effort she managed to turn on her left side. From this position she could admire the full moon, blinking from the chink between the curtains.

Out there the sky was clear and calm. Outside Nature was following her safe, normal course.

"It is here that lies the unnatural," she thought, "it is here that things don't follow their natural course, because…because of *her*." Her heart leapt. At this point there wasn't any doubt, it was all too clear. She completely unleashed her mind and the more she did so the stronger and more self-confident she felt.

"You can hit my body and you can mock my person. But my spirit is free and pure, like the moon out there."

Her mind was now wandering through the winding recesses of the mansion, up to the left wing, up to *her* room. She was standing in front of her portrait now, no more in awe and reverence this time. She felt as if she had suddenly become much older, and all her naivety had left her in the snap of a finger. The woman in the portrait had no reason, no right to feel stronger than her. The comparison with the animals in the cottage's yard came again to her mind. She could hardly understand why a harmless young lady like her could represent a threat to the proud spirit of Lady Lavinia. Nevertheless, she had been a threat and she currently was one. In the end, Lady Page was the one who was building up a privileged access to the heart of her own husband and that was enough. When she first arrived at Lastsight Hill, she was naive and pure, hardly aware of what was going on. Now she was fully aware of the situation and of her own potential as well. She had to constantly stick to this feeling of self-confidence and finally the whole figure of Lady Lavinia would be dissolved in nothingness, like melting snow. It was all a matter of her own mind. Yes, Lady Lavinia's spirit was nourished by her own indecisions and doubts. She must stop feeding her. Any hesitation of her heart could be fatal. She had to be strong.

A creak. A creeping sound coming from the door. She became alarmed, but then remembered the maid sitting outside and felt relieved. Maybe it was her, just checking that Milady was sleeping and not in need of anything. But what if the maid had fallen asleep? What if it was someone else? The muffled sound of the steps was only slightly perceivable. Maybe it wasn't human steps and there wasn't anyone at all.

...any hesitation of her heart could be fatal...

She tried to turn. What she could perceive out of the corner of her eye was a blurred shadow in the dark, nothing more. Her aching body grew paralyzed and she eventually closed her eyes and prayed. Had she been too bold in her last thoughts? Had she been too defiant?

...any hesitation of her...

A touch on her right shoulder. A soft touch.
She resolutely reopened her eyes and turned her face again, to meet the eyes of Lord K.

In his arms, she felt that her aching body wasn't aching at all and that her spirit could finally cease to be tense and on guard. At last, the moon had stepped in and brought in the reassuring breath of Nature. For a little frame of time and space, things were following a healthy natural course in Lastsight Hill.
But it couldn't last long.
The moon set and the early light of dawn brought in the first stirrings of harsh reality. She had eventually fallen asleep. He couldn't. Gazing at her rosy face, he couldn't help but dwell on her scars and marks, which made an insulting, unbearable contrast to her marble-like skin. All this aroused a mix of tenderness and anger in him. He couldn't stay still, least of all sleep. The best idea was going out with Melmoth, as usual, having a good, refreshing walk in the moors and pondering over what would be the best to do next. Walking in the open air would help.
He got up gently, careful not to awake Milady and quietly left the room. On the threshold, he had a moment of hesitation.
"Go and sit inside the room, Joanna," he bade the young maid who was just outside, "and please never leave Milady for an instant, never."

Daphne Ashby was sitting in the back of a car for the very first time in her life, crossing the whole of Yorkshire from the coast. Young Phillips and Mr Walsh were quiet most of the time, but when they started a conversation, they sounded quite animated. She didn't pay any attention to them, to tell the truth, partially because she was immersed in her own thoughts and partially because of an impending sense of sickness that had been accompanying her since the very beginning of the journey. They were now towards the end of it, a few miles from their destination and this feeling was increasing horribly.

"You look very absorbed by this case, Phillips."

"This man is noxious," he answered after a while to his brother-in-law.

"He might be," Walsh replied, looking attentively at the road beyond the steering wheel, "but in the end, in all honesty, what we have is just a bunch of conjectures, mere speculations from an overly sensitive lady we have just known during the summer. Besides," he took a pause and slightly turned towards his friend, "I thought you despised her."

"I have nothing against Mrs Monti, I just find that she is too impressionable."

"I'm not talking about her."

Young Phillips gazed at him in return and then turned carefully to the rear, where Daphne was apparently dozing off.

"You don't understand," he said in a lower tone, avoiding the hint about Lady Page. "That man is dangerous for himself and for the others around him. I had this feeling all along. It wouldn't have affected me if it weren't that the Ashby family is extremely dear to me, as is evident, and I don't want anything bad for them to happen."

"I see," Walsh said laconically, staring at the road in front of him in silence.

"But then…"

"What now?" Phillips sounded extremely irritated.

"You're surprising me, Phillips. You have never relied on this kind of thing before, I mean premonitory dreams, visions and suchlike. I thought you were sceptical about all that. After the Cotgraves episode, you were the first and only one to make fun of that lady - you said, and I quote, 'a kind old granny with the aspirations of a witch'."

"Well, this has nothing to do with what I was talking about."

"Of course it has."

"You keep not understanding, Walsh, you don't understand!" he burst out impatiently, this time raising his voice carelessly.

"Why didn't you say anything before, then?" Walsh insisted. "And why did you despise Mrs Cotgrave and Mrs Monti for saying in other words the very same things you're saying?"

"Because…oh dear," he grumbled. "First of all, nobody could really fathom what Mrs Cotgrave was referring to in her hallucinatory state, she just bade Lady Page go away, as far as we know. Secondly, as I said, I have nothing against Mrs Monti and I don't despise her. I am simply stating that she reported something completely unclear and undetailed about her fears and was just mumbling something about strange dreams. It could be anything!" He crossed his arms and looked around, exasperated. "The fact that her generic anxieties match my own strong suspicions is in the end just a pure coincidence," he added, emphasizing the last word.

"Yes, I understand, but again…"

Daphne wasn't sleeping at all. Her sickness increased mile after mile. She was leaning her head on the back seat, while the men's voices arrived confusedly at her ears and she couldn't fully grasp the meaning of their words. The smell of the car's metal frame, mixed with that of fuel, was

sickeningly intoxicating and grew worse and worse. She
didn't dare say anything. She didn't want to be a bother and
so there she was, with large marks under her eyes and her
hand pressing her stomach.

A recurring thought was hanging around her head and she
was sufficiently honest with herself to admit it: it could be
her. It could have been her in the place of her sister and
the very audacious part of this thought was in the relief she
felt. It was a very selfish feeling, but it existed, she couldn't
help it.

She recalled the disappointment she had felt when Lord K
had come to their cottage for the very first time and, while
eavesdropping on the conversation between him and her
mother, she had learned about his choice regarding Page.
It wasn't something to do with the marriage in itself. Nor
with the man, even if it's true that she had recognised in
herself a sort of fascination towards this uncommon
fellow. But in the end, she didn't care. He was a stranger to
her and she was perfectly aware that one man or another
didn't make any difference to her present situation. She had
just to accept her destiny as part of the family's assets. This
resigned cynicism was a shadowy side of Daphne that no
one knew, not even her sagacious sister. Besides, she didn't
even like this Young Phillips - he was always talking about
himself and when he wasn't, he had this unpleasant way of
looking down at people that was presumptuous enough to
get on her nerves. "The Poet Laureate", they called him.
He had built up his public image around it and yet,
according to her sister, his poems were not so great. He
had made his proposal to her in an awkward way, the night
after their visit to the Cotgraves. He hadn't even looked
into her eyes while proposing and had looked distracted.
Somehow, she had sensed that he was play-acting and she
was still asking herself why he did it. "Never mind," she

had thought, "it's an opportunity and I am growing old."

When Lord K had proposed to Page, something more subtle had upset her, something concerning her pride and a sense of having being overlooked. And look at herself now, she was engaged with Young Phillips, a wealthy and well-respected gentleman, while her sister had to deal with a sinister, probably deranged husband living in a gloomy mansion.

And yet…

Something inside herself wasn't exactly sure about what was wrong in all this.

She wasn't so certain about the malignant nature of this mysterious Lord K. In the end, nobody really knew him. She couldn't quite understand the stubborn hostility that her future husband was displaying towards him. In the same way, she could hardly understand how he was so sure that all the dangers and threats to her sister dwelt in the person of Lord K himself. Although she had somehow sensed what was going on - Young Phillips's vehemence a few hours before in underlining Lady Page's *'insane tenderness'* towards her own husband had only confirmed her suspicions. Deep inside her, it was clear that she, Daphne Ashby, had been chosen as a replacement for her sister or maybe worse: as a perverse sort of revenge. God only knew what was in Young Phillips's mind. Even now, even though her physical state was too weak to pay any attention to his words, she could perceive from his heated tone that he was talking about Lord K and her sister.

She leant her head to the side, her sickness growing, the landscape outside melting in front of her eyes. In the meantime, a sudden intuition crossed her mind while she was gasping for some fresh air from the car window. She remembered the day on which she had knocked at her sister's door, before she left the seaside. She recalled the flash in Page's eyes when she had asked her, "Where do you belong, then?" Of course. She hadn't caught the detail at that moment, because she was too selfishly involved in her engagement with Young Phillips. But now that she was thinking it over, again and again, she clearly understood. Happiness, yes. It had been a sparkle of happiness that she had detected in her sister's eyes. How could it be so if Lord K was really the portrait of evil that Young Phillips was depicting? "No one knows Lord K," she repeated to herself. No one but Page. She ought to tell her fiancé about it, she ought to tell him now. But she felt so utterly weak that she could merely close her eyes and barely tried to breathe more fresh air from the window, while the two in the front were deeply engaged in a never-ending discussion.

If they had not been so engaged and if Daphne had not been so ill, they would have realised that something was wrong in the landscape around them. They would have realised that, while on their right side Nature was florid and rich, displaying the vivacity of the departing summer and the vivid colours of the approaching autumn, on their left side trees, bushes and meadows were shrouded by a spell of death - leaves had prematurely gone in a bleak anticipation of winter, leaving gaunt and dark branches studded against a pale sky; the few plants that remained were all withered and shrivelled, while the birds had ceased to sing and the grass looked completely burnt. A grim, silent desolation had been cast on that portion of land by a hidden hand. Life seemed to have descended underground, as narrated in ancient myths about the departing summer, sucked up by the will of some deity and ready to flourish again only six months later.

But the car was proceeding along the straight white line of the road, regardless.

They were riding right on the border between Heaven and Hell, while Lastsight Hill was looming in the distance.'

CHAPTER TWELVE

PREPARATION

'Her mind came unwillingly back to her present situation. Joanna came quietly in. "Your breakfast will be served in a moment, the fire has been started in the fireplace…" she could hear her saying along with other practical things that she wasn't really paying attention to.

She turned her head towards the chink between the curtains. The moon had definitely gone and in its place the blinding sun had found its way, spotlighting the empty portion of the bed by her side.

She felt a grip in her stomach. How different it would have been to wake up together, to admire those very same sun rays caressing his opening eyelids. His absence had a taste that she didn't like, the taste of an impending danger. During these times they *must* stay together.

She made some effort to wipe her feelings away, till her breakfast was served and soon after that Mrs Haffelaw stepped in, immediately drawing the curtains aside. A creature of the daylight, of brisk manners and disciplined work, Mrs Haffelaw never showed a trace of feelings, a characteristic that was probably among the silent conditions required by her job. It is true that every house and mansion needs a housekeeper, possibly as strict and meticulous as she was. Yet, Lady Page sometimes asked herself what a being like Mrs Haffelaw had in common with Lastsight Hill and whether the housekeeper realised at the time what was going on in the household that she was running.

"Is Milady feeling better?" she asked formally.

"Yes, thank you Mrs Haffelaw, much better."

"Good."

Mrs Haffelaw hadn't displayed the slightest change in her attitude, not even after the hideous facts of the day before. The two women - bound over a house they shared, each of them playing a different role - were as different from each other as fire and earth. *Never question* was Mrs Haffelaw's creed and she overtly adhered to this principle all the time. That which couldn't find a rational explanation had to be ignored. As simple as clear water. Besides this, Lady Page had actually never met her favour. She probably was one of those persons who deservedly attracted misfortunes, like her own mother would have pontificated. And in the end, who was able to exclude the possibility that she had thrown the books by herself in a fit of hysteria, to seek a piece of attention from her sick husband? Since she had set foot in Lastsight Hill, she had brought nothing but troubles. Milord was a strange character indeed, but he was quiet and reasonable. More importantly, as long as he had been alone in his mansion, the daily routine had never been disrupted and she had been able to carry out her tasks smoothly.

"Has Milord gone with Melmoth?" Milady dared to ask, careful not to display any sign of anxiety.

"Of course, he is out with the horse, as usual." In her own language, animals didn't deserve to be called by name.

"Before he went, he said…"

"What did he say?" she couldn't help but exclaim leaning forward, betraying her feelings. Mrs Haffelaw stared at her in a puzzled way.

"He just said to make sure that Milady had her meals and recommended for you not to undertake any unnecessary physical effort."

"I feel quite better, though."

"I am just reporting what he said," she replied coldly and moved towards the door.

"I'll leave you alone with your breakfast now. If you need anything please don't hesitate to call me."

"I won't. Thank you, Mrs Haffelaw."

At the sound of the door shutting, she called at once for her maid.

"Joanna, please help me to get dressed."

The young lady looked at her, confused.

"But Mrs Haffelaw said…"

"Don't listen to Mrs Haffelaw. Please do what I said."

The maid hastened to do what she had been told, a little incredulous but somehow excited.

The bruises were still aching, true, but in the end she could easily move her limbs. The only critical points were the back of her neck, where she had received the first blow and her right side, which had been repeatedly hit by the books while she was attempting to protect her head. But as long as she didn't bend her head excessively, she couldn't feel any pain to her neck; the same with her side, unless she engaged in some odd movements. A couple of times, Joanna could hear her moaning in pain during her dressing up.

"Is Milady fine?" She would immediately worry in panic, reddening in her face.

But her mistress would look up at her and smile every time. Once finished, she tried to pace here and there in her room and found that she could manage to walk perfectly.

"I *am* fine, completely fine," she whispered, looking at herself in the mirror.

"Your hair needs to be done, Milady."

"No." She turned firmly to her maid and smiled.

"Leave it as it is."

There was a place she absolutely wanted to visit. It was the library. It exerted on her the power of a magnet. She was determined to see the scene, no matter what kind of feelings it could arouse. It wouldn't take long. Take the stairs to the first floor, turn right, third door.

In approaching the library, she could hear a rustle and a bumping noise. A thrill ran along her spine, but soon afterwards she understood that the fresh memory of the previous day was playing a bad trick on her mind. She reached the threshold decisively and saw that three maids, with the help of the young gardener Neal, were silently tidying up the mess, placing the books randomly on the shelves. She smiled at the thought that Lord K was going to be irritated by the careless way in which they were putting Shelley's poems next to the Indian Mythology and psychology treatises next to the German Gothic novels. In the end, what were they supposed to know about it? She would re-organise it herself.

At the moment she had stepped in, they had suddenly stopped and had stared at her, waiting for some likely instructions to be given. But she simply nodded and stepped backwards - better to leave them alone with their work. Yet, there was a sort of disappointment clinging to her. It would have been different to cross the threshold and to find the library completely empty. She would have walked right among the piles of gaping books, almost leaving them to observe her, as though they were living creatures - a sort of perverse ritual of re-actualisation of what she had experienced. She felt as though she *wished* they could move and twist and spin again as they had done. But the presence of other human beings had in some way broken the spell and there was no sense whatsoever in walking about among bunches of mere inanimate, inked paper spread all over the place.

Back on the landing, her gaze automatically went to the other staircase, leading to his own quarters and to the west wing - they seemed to beckon her in an unbearable way. She moved back and hastily took the last flight of stairs to the ground floor and for a moment stood all alone in the middle of the big hall, contemplating the silence. The mullioned windows were softly touched by golden rays of sun that in turn dispersed themselves in myriads of sparks once they reached the big chandelier - this magnificent piece of art came directly from the island of Murano, a little strip of land near Venice, where Lord K had practiced as a psychiatrist for some years. No one could really understand how he could have bothered to bring this bulky and fragile handiwork from such a great distance. Every single glass drop had been carefully manufactured by skilful hands hundreds of miles away and finally they had miraculously landed here in the North Riding of Yorkshire. Every single time she looked at it, it reminded her of the ball, of the very first time she had come to Lastsight Hill, a night on which she had never imagined that, one day, it would become her own house. The chandelier stood there, now as then, like a supreme witness, every hanging drop as a part of a huge jury. A draught of air arrived to brush them from time to time, making them jingle. The sound of it was soothing and disquieting at the same time.

On hearing some steps, she woke up from her brooding and moved towards the kitchens, gliding along the walls of the passages. Once there, she met the surprised eyes of the cook, but before the latter uttered any word Lady Page placed a finger on her own mouth. After that, she fetched a hamper from a cupboard and put a notebook and pencil in it, together with some food taken randomly from wherever she could reach.

"I'm doing it again," she thought, half smiling. In fact, she had done the same two days ago, soon after having come back from the seaside, acting like a stranger.

"As if I was not the owner of the house."

In a sense, it was as if Mrs Haffelaw was the real mistress and she had to be accountable to her.

And amid all this, there was the tenant of the west wing to take into account.

He had taken the usual path which led towards the bare highlands, dominated by huge rocks spread all over the place. Here he stopped and sat down with his back leaning on one of them, left Melmoth free to pasture and left his own mind free as well. The wind was whistling gently between the rocks, in a way that seemed to encourage his thoughts to arise. He closed his eyes. Damn MacAllister and his mad idea of the ball. It had all settled so well, his life had taken a routine pleasant and quiet enough to keep him satisfied. He grinned bitterly. *Satisfied*? Was that the proper term to define his state of calm sorrow? Lady Page was right. That was not happiness. It was a just life similar to "the smooth surface of the sea when no wind bewilders it", she had said in the drawing room. How miserable, how wretched. Yes, wretched, that was what he had become. Yet how could he blame himself? And then the letter from his in-law had arrived, then the idea of the ball and...and this young lady in a white dress, her brow frowned, outstanding among all the other ladies enjoying the dancing. It had been his morbid curiosity at first that had led him to follow her and the elegant chap who seemed to have disappointed her. He had guessed she was in love with him. But when he later understood who Page Ashby was, he could clearly state that it wasn't the case - how could a vain man like Young Phillips possibly get the interest of a woman like her? Then the visit to the cottage and that look she had cast at him. She had boldly stared back at him and he had felt naked, as if she could read his own feelings.

With time he had further confirmation that the woman he had taken home was far from being ordinary. They never had many occasions to talk, due to his own indications about preserving his quiet life. Yet despite this, something was creeping inside him and he had started to feel the fear. The fear of change, the fear that the sea surface of his monotonous life was not so smooth any more and was starting to ripple.

His animals had soon felt her friendly energy and he had been particularly touched by that. It wasn't precisely jealousy that he had felt, now he realised - whenever he saw Ishtar following Milady towards the hills, he couldn't help but feel that a part of him was going with them, rushing through the bushes, running along the brooks. He couldn't lie to himself any more. He had to admit he was developing a loving and caring attitude towards Lady Page. Until recently, he had been too confused to understand how to deal with all this, when the episode of the birds happened.

Then he had seriously started to be concerned, not so much with regard to his own feelings as regarding the tenant of the west wing, who seemed disappointed by the fact that he no longer attended regularly their evening meetings.

Therefore, she had launched her first attack, delivering a message that hadn't been so much directed towards Lady Page, as towards him. It said: *You're not going to understand? I will strike your beloved, then.*

That was clever indeed. It had been more effective than striking him. Did she have the right to do so to him, to *them*? As much as their bond was tight, he had begun to feel the leash strangling his throat and that was enough. Time was finally awakening him from his maddening bereavement and opening the way to reason. She was definitely crossing the line. Had he known about the hallucination caused by Lavinia's portrait he could have intervened before Lady Page accepted to leave for the seaside. She had revealed this event, among other things, the previous night, while they were together. How did Lavinia dare - it startled him when his thoughts materialised her name – how did she dare to play so unfair as to make Page re-live the distressful moment of her death and their son's death? It had been a dishonourable way to tell her "*Accept it, you will never take my place.*" And then the afternoon in the drawing room came to his mind, when Lady Page had come back from the holiday and she was so beautiful with her thoughtful face, leaning on the sofa, gradually opening her heart to him in all sincerity.

...the leash tightening and tightening...

And there s*he* had appeared, for the first time out of her quarters, imposingly. He had started to tremble like a child caught by a strict tutor.

...tightening, tightening...
And finally, the library.
That had been the ultimate red line. Something had to be done, a decision had to be taken. He could no longer allow all this to unfold. What about leaving Lastight Hill? She would have cursed them anywhere and furthermore, hard to understand, he was unexplainably affectionate towards that place and to those lands. No, he had to address the issue the other way round, *they* had to get rid of her. *She* had to go and leave them alone. But how? He had no idea how to cleanse a haunted house, despite his experience as a doctor with patients who had claimed to be possessed or to see the spirits of the dead. His approach had always been strictly medical and scientific, even though he had always been a kind of open-minded psychiatrist, keen on going off the beaten track of the official medical field. And lastly it is worth bearing in mind that in this particular case he was directly and personally involved, far from maintaining a cold scientific distance.

A gust of strong wind suddenly blew in the crick between the rocks, refreshing his mind. His pupils enlarged. He had an idea. It wasn't that much, quite simple in fact, but why hadn't he thought about it before? Her things, her belongings: let's start from them. They were all around her and preserved her energy.

He got up; Melmoth turned towards him and waved his head happily, glad to go back home.

The brook rushed by noisily and its little waves and pebbles sparkled in the clear sun of September. He decided to take the walk following its bank, instead of the usual path along the valley. At last, it was time for a change.

Cezary was heavily climbing the stairs leading to the west wing for his daily survey.

He had carefully taken off his muddy boots and attentively washed his hands before doing so - once he had been harshly scolded by Mrs Haffelaw for having the edge of his shirt slightly dirty with soil: "If you want to go to Milady's room you need to have a dignified appearance," she had said. "Go and change your shirt."

She wasn't sure he had completely understood, but after having jabbered something in his mother tongue, he had done exactly what he had been told. From then on, with a good deal of reluctance, he had always been very careful, for the sake of peace, if for anything. He simply wanted to avoid being annoyed by that old witch.

He was currently late on the schedule, as Neal had been called to give a hand in the library, leaving him alone to attend to the stables. He was internally grumbling about that, about how many things he had to manage by himself and so on, when out of the corner of his eye he saw the library door open and decided to have a glimpse - there he was, Neal, lazy lad, more interested in looking furtively at the maids than tidying up the mess. But then his gaze was caught by the general picture of the room still with a lot of volumes lying around, the shelves only half full. Look what *his* Milady had been able to do: to humble this ridiculous, spoiled young mistress in such a powerful way. She had given her the lesson she'd deserved, like that time with the birds at the glasshouse (how he had enjoyed that havoc). But Lady Page hadn't got the lesson yet. Of course she hadn't, she was stupid. What had his master to do with this insignificant young lady? He had completely lost his mind and he, Cezary, had lost all his respect towards his master - he had re-directed it all towards his Milady. In fact, he was still committed to Lastsight Hill uniquely for *her* sake. *She* was a real noble lady, towering over all the other ones - no one could ever compete with her. He could see them, whenever he went to town to buy books for his master - all these wealthy women roaming in couples or in groups, giggling nervously behind their fans any time a man passed by, chatting most probably about hairstyles and satin gloves, pointing at gowns and bonnets exposed in the shops' windows. How vastly superior was Lady Lavinia. She always had been. And this ginger haired girl was not only stupid, although she showed herself to be a writer and a book reader, she was also stubborn and insolent and had always shown a defiant attitude towards him and even towards Mrs Haffelaw. If the housekeeper had managed to remain untouched by such behaviour, it was not the same for him - he had travelled miles and crossed the sea to guard his mistress and to take care of her shrine…she should have shown more respect towards him. In that regard she was a perfect match for that lapdog MacAllister, who not only looked at him in an offensive way, but had even obtained access to the forbidden quarters, where only he, Cezary, had been admitted so far. To hire this individual had already been an unhappy step taken by his master, but at least he could tolerate him. Not the same with Lady Page. That had definitely been too much.

He had had a mild relief when she had gone away three months before. His master had been visibly saddened by this event, but hopefully – he thought – time would bring resignation and he would come back onto the old rails. And so it had happened.

Yet, with utter disappointment he had observed that his master was not exactly the same as before. That was the trouble with human beings - you can never restore them to the previous state, unlike a wall or a fence that has been damaged and which you can easily fix with an approximation very close to its old condition. If he only could fix his master! If he only could restore Lastsight Hill to its previous, almost idyllic state!

But there's always something new interposing and spoiling your plans, isn't there old Cezary? There's always something messing up the cards on the table. If only this young lady had never appeared. If only…

"Everything all right, Cezary?"

The firm voice of Mrs Haffelaw, whose figure had been unnoticed by him so far, startled him. As usual, he made no reply.

"Go to your own tasks then, there's nothing to peer at here," she said in her familiar monotonous voice.

He went, reluctantly. And as he climbed the last creaking steps to his destination he couldn't help but grin, in total contempt towards the rest of the household. Towards Mrs Haffelaw, the maids, Neal, Lady Page and, most of all, towards his master. He had far more important business to do that their petty domestic concerns.

As he inserted the key and turned it in the keyhole, his sense of pride in his role increased enormously. He stepped in, filled his lungs with the familiar smell of blood that pervaded the room and automatically found his way in the dark towards the window. A sudden blast of wind pushed the panels wide open as he released the latch.

The weather was changing.

A triumphant thought crossed his mind - the young lady, the silly ginger haired lady, was out on the moors. What a nice coincidence if she were to be caught by a sudden storm. He couldn't help exchanging a glance of complicity with the portrait on his right side, while the curtains swayed to and fro at the ever-changing gusts of wind. A couple of ribbons rolled onto the floor, the mannequin with her dark frock wavered, losing the scarlet shawl a little bit on one shoulder, the diary on the desk spread open and the pages turned madly. He clumsily managed to restore everything to its place as best he could.

At that moment he had had the strange impression that *the room was alive* and, to be completely honest with himself, it wasn't such a pleasant feeling - he was used to the blood smell, he could contemplate dispassionately what his Milady had been able to inflict on others, but the simple sight of her belongings moving around in her room literally chilled his backbone. In all this, the portrait had remained stock-still on its nail, not swaying an inch, as though it was the necessary steady agent which, by the help of its inner force, had provoked all the mess in lieu of the wind.

For the first time, the affectionate feelings he had towards his Milady gave way to something quite close to what is commonly called terror.

Then he wisely understood that it was time to shut the windows again. In awe of the portrait, he awkwardly hinted a bow and slowly stepped backwards towards the door, never losing sight for a moment of her cold, magnetic eyes. He didn't have time to notice that the scarlet shawl on the mannequin had disappeared.'

CHAPTER THIRTEEN

ENDGAME

'Ishtar was sniffing happily at the moss and the wet fallen leaves, never losing track of her human companion. Page's foot slipped in the muddy turf from time to time, re-awakening the pain in her side. But she persisted, scanning the horizon ahead.

"If they are not there, they should be beyond that slope. At any rate, from there I can survey everywhere around."

The sun was high but the air was crisp and thin white clouds swept along fast. Page and Ishtar reached the top of the hill and descended the slope, but there was no trace of Lord K, nor of Melmoth.

"How strange," she thought.

She had come along the way that he usually took both to go to and to come back from the moors and he wasn't there. This variation in his routine was particularly unusual for a methodical person like him.

She put her hamper down on the ground and decided to

have a rest, forcing herself to eat some of the food, while Ishtar was busy searching for little creatures.

Not far from them, on their left side, stood a small aspen thicket, deeply entangled in a vast expanse of bramble. In front of her, the valley spread out, dotted all over the place with scattered rocks. Now, without the presence of the beloved whom she had hoped to find, they assumed a sinister look that so far she had never noticed. The ominous feeling creeping inside her was reinforced by a rising breeze that was hollowly whistling among the rocks, resulting in eerie sounds.

After consuming her meal, she lay down on the grass with a sigh and started to contemplate the moving sky, lulled by the rustle of the brambles waving in the wind.

"Try not to think for a moment, Page," she whispered to herself, "try not to be concerned. You're far from her place. You're safe, like a bird in its den, like a mole in a niche in the ground. In a niche in the ground…"

The exquisite feeling of the soil touching her skin crossed the border with her unconscious, reaching her dreamy state. There she was, lying on the ground, deep into the ground. Cezary was staring at her and from far away she could hear heavy noises, like a tool hitting something hard. Lord K hitting the door of the glasshouse? She could hear him calling for her but she couldn't move a limb, nor answer back. On the sky above – above the hollow in which she lay – she could see the white stripes of the clouds scudding by madly, until they grew darker and even changed their shape. "Oh no, not again...," then they scattered in black fragments – birds flying - and the sunshine flickered on her eyes behind the dance of dark feathers. The thuds grew louder and louder, annoying to her ears. Suddenly, they took a strange tone, definitely not the metallic sound of a tool hitting a thick panel of glass.

They were…they were barks.

Ishtar was barking spasmodically by her side, quite close to her ears.

"What's wrong?"

She blinked her eyes. Her emerging consciousness was struggling with the flickering effect of the sun's rays through the clouds. She screened her eyes with her hand, trying to hush Ishtar, and discovered that it wasn't a conspiracy of ravens, nor the striped white clouds that were perturbing the light, but something else: a long, floating object, apparently reddish. She wasn't able to identify it. It swung from here to there, pushed aloft by the conflicting gusts of wind that had increased in strength and were now almost howling among the rocks.

"Stop talking, go faster!"

The two gentlemen, astonished, went quiet immediately.

Her distressed face beckoned from the rear mirror - she looked utterly dismayed and impatient.

"Miss Ashby, are you all…"

"I said stop talking and go," she burst out. "There's no time to waste, just go!"

Young Phillips, who had now turned towards Daphne, remained speechless. He then exchanged a glance with Mr Walsh, "Haven't you heard her? Move!"

Walsh didn't say a word. He obediently trod on the accelerator and the vehicle darted through the silent countryside like a marble thrown by a child through a furrow in the flat white sand.

"These Ashby sisters are really intriguing," Young Phillips thought with half a smile, while he glanced furtively at her red-rimmed eyes in the rear mirror.

The floating object had caught her eyes and her attention.

She sprang up and slowly paced towards it, while Ishtar hadn't ceased barking for a moment, sticking her paws firmly onto the ground.

"Hush, it's nothing!"

But the dog wouldn't obey her this time.

The mysterious thing flew to the right, then the wind drove it aloft, then it twirled to the left and finally fell down to suddenly start the dance again.

She couldn't detach her eyes from it - the enchantment it played on her had something familiar about it, a feeling she should have recognized at once.

But the sun was shining so pleasantly and the smell of the countryside came so fragrantly to her nostrils, that nothing else mattered. Everything was confused as if she was living in a prolonged state of her dream, like in a melting down of colours and sensations - the wet bark of the trees, the purple of the heather, the hard white of the rocks, Ishtar's voice in the distance.

And eventually, the reddish stripe was guiding the rhapsody, upward and downward, twirl and turn.

She was walking through the pastures, trying to catch it.

Thousands of multicoloured leaves seemed to join the rhapsody, twirling and dancing. She proceeded and her side was aching and her neck was in pain in the effort of stretching her hands and body towards the sky.

"Never mind the pain, I'll catch it soon."

And her feet seemed lighter and lighter, touching a ground that – had she given a glance behind her back – instantly got darker and bleaker at every step, as though in her rapture she was sucking up the life from the meadows and the trees and bushes around her.

Furious barks in the distance. And a final whimper.

She finally grabbed it. What a refined object - its delicate fabric slipped gently among her thin fingers. Its colour was of an intense kind of crimson. And suddenly the sense of familiarity arrived with a stab to her heart, along with the pungent odour coming from it.

She instantly knew she had smelled that scent before. A flash of understanding crossed her mind - blood, the shawl on the mannequin, Milady's room. Before she knew it, the shawl had wrapped around her wrists and dragged her across the land.

Ishtar's eyes were following her human companion in utter frustration. Her nervous paws were just moving frantically from side to side, not daring to go forward and to trespass the invisible line dividing her from Lady Page. What was she doing down there? Why was she engaged in such a bizarre chasing game and was she, Ishtar, supposed to join in? She really couldn't fathom why her lady was walking weirdly to and fro, sometimes stumbling on the rocks and bumping into them, uttering dismal moans.

But she was afraid. *That* was the only thing that she could clearly understand.

And that's why she found it impossible to move forward. She could smell her own fear.

The land in front of her, beyond that invisible line, was dark and lifeless. She could sense it very distinctively now, as even the birds had fled away, abandoning all the gaunt and bare trees over there to find refuge in the luxuriant trees behind her.

It was that floating thing. Yes. She sensed that her lady's strange behaviour had something to do with the object that was now tightly tied around her wrists and arms. She had seen many times her dear lady wearing things like this in the same fashion and she loved sniffing at their hems, they had such a lovely smell about them. Yet, this time she had divined it was somewhat evil, since the very first moment she had seen it floating about the horizon. However, she couldn't make anything of it and her perplexities were increasing. What should she do? Did she have to cross the border and take any action? Or was she supposed to leave her alone? Maybe she had to wait for a command from her. Yes, maybe that was the right thing to do. But she felt that something was wrong, something was transgressing the normal 'obey-sit-follow me' course of command. She was confused and frustrated. And she loved her.

"Gather all the maids and servants in the hall, immediately. Where are Cezary and Neal?"

Mrs Haffelaw stared at him apprehensively. He had stepped in hastily, he hadn't even bothered to take off his boots, which were now leaving horrible muddy prints on the just-cleaned carpet.

"They are all in the library, Milord, tidying up the mess and Cezary should be in the front gardens by now."

He rushed outside and took the main front steps of the mansion, the huge tongue of Shiva-the-Destroyer. Cezary was right there next to the glasshouse, collecting all the fallen leaves in small heaps.

"Leave it!"

The servant looked up at him puzzled - there was something in his Master's manners and tone that he didn't like at all. Lord K shouted something in his mother tongue, then snapped, "Leave this task at once and come inside the house. I need all of you. Let me explain everything in one go, to you and the others as well."

"But…"

"You can understand English, can't you?"

That was awkward. It had never happened before. The harshness of his master's last words echoed in the wind rustling among the trees above them. He stared at him

outraged, yet the angry tears in his eyes wouldn't shed.
"Do what I told you, then."

"Milord."
Mrs Haffelaw voice, calling from the distance, broke the
frozen layer between the two. She had stood at the top of
the steps for a while before calling him, contemplating the
exchange between her master and his servant. She couldn't
hear their words of course, but whatever it was about, the
tension was palpable - she didn't like the way in which they
were looking at each other and she didn't like the way in
which Cezary was gripping his rake.
"*No good,*" she thought and an inexplicable fear mixed with
anxiety began to creep all through her solid, rational
person.
They both turned towards her.
"The servants are all gathered in the hall, Milord."

All lined up they stood, staring at their master with
incredulous eyes, sometimes peering at Mrs Haffelaw's
face, whose mask of solidity had begun to crack under the
pressure of her anxiety.
"I want you all to bring down everything that is in Milady's
room. I mean the one in the west wing, the one that has
been always forbidden to you except to Cezary. You will
take down every single item, clothes, furniture, and
jewellery. Not even a bead or a nail has to remain there.
You will gather all of this at a point on the main lawns,
right in front of the entrance. I want to see the heap from
these windows. When everything is collected Neal will set
the fire."
Cezary enlarged his eyes and started to breathe heavily.
"Joanna and the other maids will take care of clothes,
garments and light objects, while you, Neal and Cezary…,"

his eyes rested on his servant's face, "…you two will take care of the heavy ones."

A strange feeling was winding among all of them, an unprecedented sensation. It was the first time that they had seen their master behaving in such a way, pacing and gesticulating in excitement, talking with a tremulous tone in his voice and gazing at them with lively eyes, as if…as if he was alive.

"Move now."

Off they went. Except one.

"Cezary." Lord K looked into his eyes and he did the same in return.

"We must do it. Please, go with the others."

A slight bow. "Yes, Milord."

Because in the end he was his master and he had to obey.

She lay on her stomach. Her ankles were in pain, after all the times she had stumbled on the smallest scattered stones around, while her face and head were suffering from the bumps on the biggest rocks. The shawl was still gripping her wrists, but it was lying harmless on the grass now, taking the shape of a hideous grin. She was panting heavily, but at least it seemed over. With a strain, she lifted her head and looked at the sulky grey sky and at the landscape around her. It was all so preposterous. All the colours had gone. And so had the birds, the leaves and the flowers.

The only colour she could perceive was the scarlet shawl in front of her eyes.

She could hear the wind gusting through the cracks in the rocks. And then there was Ishtar, barking and whimpering incessantly. She didn't have a memory of Ishtar being as overprotective and desperate during her whole residence in Lastsight Hill, as she was now. Nevertheless, the dog stood on the spot by the slope, restrained by something she was afraid of.

Lady Page tried to call her, in vain.

She rested her head on the ground and began to breathe deeply, trying to recover. She even closed her eyes, until she felt a pull on her wrists. It had started again. That hideous shawl had started its job again. It was lifting her whole body from the ground and took the opposite direction, dragging her in such a way that she was facing the sky and was brushing the soil with her heels.

"Where are you...?" but she couldn't finish. Her voice had gone again.

Ishtar's voice instead became more and more audible. The red thing was dragging her towards the dog.

She was jumping on the spot, her paws as tense as ever. She had never been so scared in all her young life, not even that time she had ventured to go inside the stables. On that occasion, she had been wandering around Gemma, who was not as docile and friendly as Melmoth. The mare had snorted grumpily, tossing her head with jerky and threatening movements towards the dog. From then on, Ishtar had never dared to explore the stables any more. But that was different. She somehow knew what it was about the other animals - once you get accustomed to their behaviour you can predict their reactions and act accordingly. But how could you deal with *this*?

She couldn't leave her lady there in the same way as she had left the stables. That red thing looked so much like a snake floating in the sky. How many times had she met snakes and vipers while wandering about the countryside - she knew very well that it was better to stay away from them, yet her experience told her that snakes don't fly, and in any case, this one looked much more wicked than those slithering on the ground. And now it was dragging her human companion closer and closer to her. Was it an act of surrender and mercy? Was it coming to hand her lady to her? How she wished to understand! Then, she realised that her friend and the thing dragging her were not coming straight to her now – instead, they were taking the way on her left. She looked to her side and again towards them and again to her left side until a flash of understanding crossed her pure heart and she suddenly clenched her jaws, her ears pointing to the sky, her paws tense. A growl was mounting deep in her throat. Yes, to her it was now clear what was next and where it was about to happen - at the aspen thicket. In particular, the huge, spiky, monster-like bramble.

"Ouch," her soft cry was hardly audible.
The shawl had dropped her heavily on the bed of brambles and the thorns mercilessly pierced her body, digging deeper and deeper in her flesh as she sank into them. Yet she couldn't feel their stings, as her whole body was aching and the diffuse feeling of pain induced in her a sort of blessed state. So must have felt hermits and saints whom she had read about in Lord K's library, after they had endured all sorts of self-inflicted deprivations and challenges. She hadn't chosen this, though. But she could now fully comprehend what they were pursuing in the harshness of deserts and forests, and their choice suddenly seemed less bizarre there on a bed of thorns than it had while reading about them in the comfort of a heated library, sitting in a comfortable chair. She felt next to Paradise. *"After this test, I can endure any trial,"* she thought.
"Will there be an *after*?" she murmured under her breath.
This sudden awareness dawned as sharp as the thorns injuring her body. She hadn't considered that.
Her head leant against a tree, her chin bent over her chest

and her arms rested on her lap so that her inanimate torturer was once again in front of her.

Right at that moment, her tormentor started to move again. It gently lifted her hands a few inches and it was so tight between them, that her wrists seemed to be bleeding from time to time. Then, the shawl came closer and closer to her chest and her chin, closer to her throat. She could feel the pressure of the fabric on her delicate skin and her trachea.

Ishtar was still barking nervously at the foot of the bramble, caught by instinctive fear and indecision, jumping to and fro, in a sort of incessant hysterical dance, until she witnessed another step in the escalating crisis - the hands of her human friend were slowly moving backward, towards her own face. And that hideous red thing was still there. The flying snake had stopped flying and was now so close to her friend that it pressed her throat and made her eyes roll. Was she calling for help? The spiky bramble looked grotesque. Now it was even starting to move, it seemed, as if animated by an inner force, until thorny branches sprang out of it, like snakes coming out of their dens. One by one, with horrific snaps, they wrapped the whole body of Milady. The last snake-like branch mercilessly crossed her friend's face, running over her left eye. At the peak of her irresolution and dread, Ishtar could do nothing but rely on her instinct, which made her utter a loud, prolonged howl.

The column of smoke rising from the heap gave him a mixture of relieving and disquieting feelings. The mannequin bent crooked and disfigured under the effect of the flames and the wood of the furniture was crackling noisily. The last death rattle.

"Finally," he sighed. And yet a feeling of uncertainty was

pervading his heart. He had to go out to the moors and find her and he had to do that as soon as possible. Lady Page was in danger out there. What kind of force was riveting him to the spot? He had to move, he knew that. And yet…

He stared at the blazing heap, incapable of reasoning. His eyes were wandering from the gowns and the furniture consumed by the flames to the flickers and ashes reaching the sky. The greenhouse and the trees behind were undulating in the heat. Something was missing. Something that he was supposed to see in the scene and that wasn't there. All the servants were around the fire now, their cheeks red from the heat and the fatigue, their eyes enraptured by the magnetism of the flames devouring all the belongings that once had been the object of his love and devotion. Everything had been done. No need to rush now, they had finished their job and they could now remain there and contemplate the proceeding of that macabre ritual. Just as he was doing there, from behind the panel of the mullioned windows of Lastsight Hill. But his heart really could find neither rest nor relief.

Suddenly, he knew. He rushed outside.

"Where is the portrait?" he asked abruptly.

They exchanged gazes, but no one answered.

"Where is the portrait?"

"Cezary was supposed to bring it down, sir," the timid voice of Neal echoed from behind him, breaking the silence.

"And where is he?" He had turned towards the young servant. In his voice, there was no trace of impatience now. Just premonition.

The lad looked firmly at him and swallowed.

"I suppose he's still there."

His master sprinted towards the house.

214

"Go with him!" Joanna, the youngest maid, decisively ordered Neal, who had remained there, petrified.

In that eternal fragment of time, spasmodically extended by the pull of death, her desperate struggle for life gave way to an ecstatic resignation.

They often say that during the last moments of life, right before leaving this world, your whole past flows in front of your eyes, from your first perplexities and marvels as a child to your latest concerns and fears as an adult. For Lady Page, it was the other way round. Her mind was totally absorbed by a premonition of the future, her entire person engulfed by a glimpse of the land of shadows expecting her and she knew she wouldn't be in good company. The faceless dark-gowned Lady loomed somewhere in the moors and out of the corner of her eye Page Ashby was able to detect her imposing profile studded against the black and white landscape, like a vision inscribed in another vision.

The landscape was breathing as a whole creature. The wind was his breath, changing the tone from shouts to whispers, from whistles to howls.

She had fallen into the trap.

"So that's what death looks like. That's how I'm going to die, strangled by my own hands, sinking into a bed of thorns."

The flames were dying and what remained of Lavinia's most personal belongings was reduced to an unrecognizable mess. Yet their eyes were still riveted on the grim spectacle in front of them. The previous sense of relief had vanished - their master had gone, up to Milady's room, and they knew the quiet would soon be broken. An ominous silence was looming above them like a huge, invisible hand pressing their heads down. They were unable even to look each other, their eyes mesmerised by the crumbling, smoking heap.

And then Joanna dared to lift her eyes and casually intercepted Mrs Haffelaw's - the housekeeper's pale face had twisted in a terrified grimace, losing all her usual control, her quivering lips trying to say something but incapable of uttering any sound. The young maid traced Mrs Haffelaw's gaze back to its object, till she had turned exactly towards the same point - there in the medieval tower crowned by the dark ever-scudding clouds, leaning at the wide-open window, the mistress of the house stood triumphant, the secret Lady to whom all of them - unconsciously or not - had always been faithful.

Her white skin was shining, her smile was enchanting as well as fiendish.

It might have taken a second for them to kneel down in prostration, had her figure not tilted awkwardly forward. Now she was falling down onto the lawns of her mansion, not with the grace of a feather but with the awkwardness of a heavy human body, until a thump was heard, an earthly sound that awoke them all from their stupor. They quietly came closer to the spot and all they saw was Cezary's body over the great portrait of his one and only mistress.

Lord K rushed into Lavinia's room followed by Neal. The shutters were madly bumping the frame under the force of the wind, particularly fierce at that high corner of the west wing.

He looked down and what he saw, framed by the horrified eyes of his servants, went beyond any of his imaginings. But no hesitation took place in that fatal moment. Instead, an unprecedented determination took hold of his heart and mind.

"Fetch Melmoth and get him ready for a ride," he said to

Neal.

"What shall we do with him, sir?" the lad stuttered while pointing at the corpse underneath.

"There's no time for him now." He grabbed Neal's shoulders. "We have to think about the living."

He snatched the reins from Neal's hands and in a moment was on Melmoth's back, riding quickly through the rear exit of the mansion. Any hesitation or misty thought was wiped away - one clear intent was guiding him: finding her. And putting an end to all this.

He automatically took the usual path, but a dreadful feeling was rising up inside him. Something was wrong in the landscape, something disquieting was slithering among the heathers and the pastures. He hesitated and gradually stopped his horse. He looked all around and frowned, bewildered. The sky was turning from the orange, golden shades of the west to the discoloured, dim lights of the east, embellished by the grey-blackish vegetation underneath. The whole horizon seemed to be caught by an unnatural madness.

There was a kind of perverse fascination in all that sight - the compelling allure of marvels that go beyond any law of Nature.

And he was stuck there, incapable either of giving a rational explanation to it or of turning his gaze away, towards the reassuring, usual colours of the west. It was magnetic. Was he supposed to plunge into the grim landscape or to run away from it?

But if he was uncertain about what to do, not so was Melmoth - he was pawing the ground with impatience, ready to spring forward. He knew exactly where to go.

"Lead me there," Lord K whispered in his ears.

And off they went, following the white path leading to the

bleak, colourless realm.

"Is Mr Ba…"

"Bachmeier."

"Is Mr Bachmeier joining us for dinner?"

"I suppose he's changing his suit after the long journey from the village. He will be with us soon," Mary Ann said in a toneless voice. She was avoiding her friend's eyes, fumbling absent-mindedly with her fork on the table. On her plate she saw only apprehension.

"Mrs Ashby, she is not in any danger."

The low and yet categorical voice of Mrs Monti brought her back to her consciousness.

She slowly put her fork down and stared inquisitively at her friend, whose eyes were closed and whose hands were gently lying parallel on the table alongside her plate.

"What do you mean, Madam? You're confusing me - earlier you were saying that Page was in danger." She paused and stared at her exasperated, before starting again, louder, "You even made my elder daughter rush over there, along with Mr Walsh and Young Phillips, and now you're telling…"

"I apologize for the delay, ladies, I…"

"Not now, Mr Bachmeier!"

Her unexpected command, accompanied by a furious look, left him shocked. He stopped at the threshold, stunned. Mrs Ashby had never treated him like that before. Even the servants had stopped what they were doing. "What do you mean, Mrs Monti, for God's sake?"

Mary Ann grabbed both her hands and bent towards her, their faces so close to each other, the silence so thick around them, that she could almost hear her friend's heartbeat.

"God takes no part in it, Madam," she went on with her

eyes closed, unperturbed. "I meant what I said, as simple as that - your daughter is not in any danger now, all her troubles are finished."

With a deep sigh of relief, Mary Ann leaned back on her chair and liberating tears started to flow profusely down her cheeks.

"Can I come in now?"

"Of course you can, Mr Bachmeier. Will you pardon me?" She got up and left the room.

"As soon as I arrive, off she goes. I never thought I could have such a negative effect on people. By the way, my name is Rudolph Bachmeier, pleased to meet you, Mrs…"

"Monti. Please forgive Mrs Ashby, Mr Bachmeier. I guess she simply needs some time for herself after all this tension. I assume you know what is going on."

"Of course, Madam. I'll tell you more. I might sound a little bit rough, shall I say - people often confuse my humour with lack of sensibility. Yet, in the end, I would define myself as a melancholic of my own kind. '*I have neither the scholar's melancholy, nor the lover's,*' as the quote goes. What I mean is a sort of…"

"…humorous sadness?"

"Mrs Monti, you amaze me," he lightened up with a large smile. "Now I will surprise you in turn. I have a quality."

"And what is this quality, Mr Bachmeier?"

"I can recognise a pure heart when it's in front of me."

"I see."

"Please, Mrs Monti, I can read your mind. Don't be quick in judgment. I am not flattering you. In spite of my saying that I can recognise a pure heart when in front of me, nobody could rule out that you might exhibit a pure heart just because you are in front of me."

"You are confusing me, Mr Bachmeier."

"Indeed."

He leant forward, coming closer to her face and almost whispering, "Few people care about that family as I do. For no particular interest of mine, if you understand what I mean. I am not bothered if they despise me."

"I wouldn't say they despise you at all, Mr Bachmeier. I would say, you are a pure heart." He smiled again, enchanted.

"Now, Mrs Monti, enough of talking about this foolish bachelor man showing off his sensibility. From what I know, you seem to have – how shall I call it? - a gift. Please, tell me more. Tell me what you know."

Meanwhile in another room, after the initial relief, Mary Ann started to be tortured by doubts. Mrs Monti's sentence was echoing in her mind with all its ambiguity.

"All her troubles are finished."

He could have recognised it among thousands of others. Ishtar's howling penetrated his heart like a warm wave, a desperate plea for help that resounded with frustration, maybe even with blame. He couldn't help but shed a tear while riding wildly through the countryside - he could have set off earlier, he had waited too long.

It was Lavinia's plan: she had kept him on her leash until the end, using all the means left in her power. She had kept his mind clouded, wrapped by her enchantment of jealousy and perverse attachment. But eventually, she had pulled the leash too tight, until it had snapped and he had experienced at last the freedom of his own mind.

Ishtar's voice was coming from a faraway thicket, beyond the pastures. No need to give Melmoth directions, the horse perfectly knew he had to follow the dog's howling. He didn't know why, he was simply aware in his animal instinct that he had to follow it and that it was a good thing to do.

But once they had turned the side of the hill and crossed the bleak meadows, the dog had suddenly ceased to howl and the choking feeling in Lord K's throat increased until he felt he was unable to breathe.

And there she was, a white scarred body lying inert on the top of a thick bramble. The dog was crouching sternly at her feet, scarred all over as well, rivulets of blood dripping between her eyes down onto her muzzle. Her body language showed no enthusiasm towards her master. She stood there overprotective towards her human treasure, her tail rhythmically tapping the spiky floor.

He jumped off and ran towards the brambles. Ishtar started to growl suspiciously, but as Lord K came closer and closer, her suspiciousness gave way to recognition and affection. She awkwardly attempted to climb down the bush, getting hurt again on her paws and stomach as she limped towards him.

"They are back."

As her cheeks were gradually regaining life, crossed by subtle lines of violet, so it was with the heathers, as one by one their purple tops gradually spread across the countryside like fresh blood in dried veins.

"The colours are back," she whispered again, attempting a smile.

"And she's definitely gone," he whispered back. "How could you possibly stand up and resist her?"

"It wasn't me, Milord. If it was for me, I'd be in the kingdom of shadows by now."

He looked at her baffled. She was barely breathing out her words with the last drops of voice left in her abused body. And she was so oddly beautiful, her white skin embroidered by her grievous injuries, her curls spread all over the place, tangled in the thorns.

"It wasn't me. It was her." Ishtar was silently surveying the landscape all around and when she felt their eyes on her, she stared back at them confused, her ears pricked in alarm, but eventually started to wag her tail and to come closer to them.

Lord K eventually noticed the gnarled shawl. Colourless and torn, it lay harmless by the side of the tree. He grabbed the massive head of the dog and kissed her between her eyes, right there where the blood rivulets were now dried and shiny.

"I can see it."

Daphne Ashby poked her head out of the car window.

Lastsight Hill was looming ahead. Its profile standing out on the skyline caught her eye like a vision, curiously brooding and endearing at the same time.

Her face was devastated by the sickness and her hairstyle had completely gone, with flecks of blondish hair waving loosely in the wind. Yet her face was strangely glowing and her heart felt lighter with relief at the idea of being finally there - until she noticed the column of smoke, when her smile faded away.

"What is it? Please, Mr Walsh, hurry up, look at that!"

He pushed the gears, while Young Phillips was looking ahead puzzled. As they approached the gate, they detected a group of people gathered by the fire and at the sound of the motor Neal and Joanna rushed towards the gateway.

"Open the gate, now! I'm Miss Daphne Ashby, can't you see? Your mistress's sister," she shouted authoritatively from the window.

The noisy car arrived as an out-of-place apparition in the remote and timeless location of Lastsight Hill. It rumbled along the gritty driveway. The servants looked on Daphne with suspicion. But after an initial reluctance, her command had a compelling effect on them and the car eventually passed through the gate.

As they pulled over in front of the entrance, Daphne got out immediately and before the servants could reach her she bent forward and threw up. Young Phillips came over, apologetic. "Miss Ashby, are you all right?"

She slowly got up, dead pale and with deep shadows encircling her eyes. Careless of Young Phillips, she turned towards the maids.

"Where's my sister?"

"She's there," Joanna pointed to the horse that was coming through the front gate. Page Ashby was riding on Melmoth's back, while Lord K was walking at her side, holding the reins. Having seen the car approaching the mansion, they had decided to follow it and to come in through the main entrance, instead of taking the back one.

"Oh my God," Young Phillips groaned. His eyes instantly caught her dress, torn apart all over the place and her face…what about her face…it was showing the clear ravages and bruises of a confrontation, not to mention the scar that crossed her left eye and the visible red mark on her throat. It was too much, outrageous to say the least. His gaze went from Lady Page to Lord K and the conclusion was soon drawn. His brow furrowed and his teeth clenched in fury. He came closer to the pair, pointing his finger at Lord K.

"You," he hissed, "you are the cause of all that. Since you arrived here you…"

"You'd better leave us alone."

It was Lady Page speaking. He was so focussed on Lord K that he hadn't noticed her slowly climbing down from the horse. At her unexpected words, he fell silent.

Without waiting for any reaction from him she moved tottering towards her dear sister, with the assistance of Mrs

Haffelaw, who at the sight of her mistress had come promptly to her aid. Lord K watched the scene attentively, unperturbed by Phillips' provocations.

The latter stood immobilized on the spot. The servants gathered by the fire were staring at him almost defiantly, while Mr Walsh, abashed, stood by the side of his car, not knowing what to make of it all.

The two sisters hugged warmly and silently cried for joy. Then Page hinted at the mansion and, with Mrs Haffelaw on one side and Daphne on the other, she started a painful climbing of the steps, when a sudden shout called them all back.

"Page Ashby! You...you don't deserve all this, you can't live with this parody of a man - look what he has done to you!"

With some difficulty, she disengaged from the grip of the two ladies and turned around. Softly her voice came, gentle but categorical.

"You should speak for yourself, Eugene Phillips."

He remained speechless.

"I warn you for the last time, leave us alone."

He looked in rapture at her, caught in a delicious mix of awe, horror and ecstasy.

This woman was a goddess, an eerie kind of goddess, and the scars that disfigured her skin simply enhanced the scandalous beauty emanating from her person. Soon a legend would spread among the youth of ******, namely that if you stared at her scarred left eye you could turn to stone, like the victims of the mythical Medusa. The legend would be put about by Lady Page's little brother Donovan, in the smart attempt to keep away the too curious children of the village, who would roam about Lastsight Hill searching for creepy adventures. She would become a source of terrifying awe then. It would never be so for

Young Phillips. Presently, had he been able to, he would have prostrated himself at her feet in worship, but he could do nothing other than stagger back, clinging to the banister to prevent himself from tumbling down.

Her stare was fierce behind the ravages, her thorn-interwoven hair waved in the wind of the moors and the house loomed over her, no more as Shiva-the-Destroyer but as a supreme protector. She was the house and the house was her. The two merged and identified. No matter who else had occupied the mansion previously, she was the one who possessed its very soul, the one who had decisively wiped out any possible contending rival, the one who haunted and who would haunt the place from that moment on.

Such awareness crossed Young Phillips' mind with indisputable clarity. He understood that his part in this play was over, that he had to leave her alone, in her divine inaccessibility.

Daphne arrived at his side and pulled his arm - "Come away, move." She brought him decisively towards the car, where he obediently took his seat, quiet as a schoolboy.

Mr Walsh, standing by the car window, kept frantically asking him questions, about what to do next and where to go. But Young Phillips wouldn't answer - he had fallen prey to a deep trance-like state that was sweetly enwrapping his senses. While Lady Page was crossing the entrance of Lastsight Hill, followed by Lord K, the young poet softly murmured:

"It's not over."

"What? What did you say, Phillips?"

"It's not over, it's not over," he carried on saying with a blank face.

And right at that moment, a blast was heard.

She grasped Mr Bachmeier's arm.

"The storm is arriving."

"Which storm, madam? The sky is completely clear and the sea is unbelievably quiet."

They stood by the terrace on the front. The landscape wasn't giving any sign of turbulence at all.

"I see, you are having another of your fits, madam, one of the kinds I witnessed in the hall with Mrs Ashby. We have to say her distressed mind is very suggestible at the moment. Well, please don't take it personally, but I am a sceptical and rational fellow, don't expect me to have the same response. I've been thinking about what you told me - what can I say? Suggestions, feelings, thoughts...sometimes they get strengthened by the power of mere coincidence. However, the least I can do is to support you in some way, despite my creed. ....may I dare to hold your hands?"

But she wouldn't listen to the rational blabbering of Bachmeier or to his attempts at flirtation.

She stepped forward and let her eyes roam across the sea. There, beyond the still line of the horizon, the wind was stirring. She could smell it. It made her feel dizzy.

"Mrs Monti," Mr Bachmeier turned unexpectedly serious.

"Nothing good," she sighed, anticipating him.

"But...Page Ashby is safe, isn't she? I remember this morning you said..."

She staggered and fainted to the floor.

"It's from within!"

Mrs Haffelaw was trying in vain to shut one of the huge windows of the hall.

"The wind is coming from within the house!"

Everyone rushed to help in stopping the window frames from bumping madly. Not Lady Page who, since the moment Mrs Haffelaw had released her arm to run towards the windows, had been standing right in the middle of the hall, staring at the top of the stairs. The housekeeper was right - the cold, threatening wind wasn't a natural atmospheric agent coming from her adored moors. On the contrary. It was a hostile, fierce blast coming from the house, coming down directly from Milady's room. And it was unnatural, it was unearthly.

Lavinia wasn't gone. She had deceived them.

From her empty room, she was still able to keep all of them in her grip.

"You won't triumph," Lady Page whispered defiantly, while all around her the house was in turmoil.

"Block the entrance, Neal! And you," Lord K pointed to Mr Walsh, who in the meantime had hastened to the house together with Daphne, while Young Phillips had remained seated in the car, stuck in his trance-like state, "you come along and help!" Lord K himself was struggling with the windows. It was as if the house had turned into an untameable, uncontrolled creature and no effort was able to rein it in. It kicked, it twisted, it even hissed through the numerous crystal drops of the chandelier, producing a disquieting, blood-chilling jingling.

The chandelier was swaying dreadfully under the force of it.

Lady Page couldn't hear any sound, neither the shouts coming from the ones around her nor the tinkling sound of the chandelier swaying over her head. In her mind, she was surrounded by dozens of couples dancing merrily to the music.

...*Swoosh...swoosh...*

The ladies' skin was bright and shiny under the light of the chandelier.

...*Swoosh...swoosh...*

The gentlemen were smiling at their partners.

…Swoosh…swoosh…

And they were all enjoying their time. Blooming youth unaware of the hidden dangers of life.

…Swoosh…swoosh…

Their eyes were glowing, their gowns and outfits were brushing the floor, all their faces were light-hearted and joyful.

All their faces, but one.

At the top of the stairs, in front of the performing band, a governess-like lady stood motionless.

…Swoosh…swoosh…

It was hard to admit how beautiful she looked, regardless of her simple attire and her plain features. Her skin was bright, her dark hair was gathered in a bun. A coarse brown gown enhanced her slim figure, a necklace made of white pearls was her only ornament.

Lady Page looked up at her in admiration, as she had looked in admiration at Lavinia's portrait, back then. Yet, now was different, deeply different. Lavinia was there with them. She was real. She felt that she could have even touched her, had she stretched her hands.

"I was wrong. You triumph."

…Swoosh…swoosh…snap.

Daphne's shriek overcame the tumult and once again silence prevailed over the child of the moors, over Lastsight Hill.

Blood and crystals.

The wind had eventually ceased to blow and the creature was now tamed.

The bulk of the chandelier had engulfed them both like an enormous crab made of glass. Lord K's body was transfixed all over the place by its pointed crystal claws. One of them had penetrated his throat. He had pushed

Lady Page to the floor and protected her with his body in an extreme attempt to save her life, to the cost of his own. And now, Lady Lavinia was content. She had disappeared from the scene. What was now blowing through the empty carcass of Lastsight Hill, coming from the still open windows, was the natural, gentle breeze of the moors, soothing to the senses.

In the sorrowful silence that followed, Mrs Haffelaw came closer, turned his body and mercifully closed his eyes.'

MILADY'S ROOM

EPILOGUE

The dust was gathering along the window frame. Mrs Haffelaw was forbidden from entering that room and Page was too fatigued by her time spent gardening to trouble herself with dusting. And above all, she was eager to read the letter. Whoever could possibly send a letter to Lastsight Hill? And to whom? Her family was visiting her regularly and she didn't have close friends. She left the window, from where her gaze had embraced the horizon, and finally sat on the armchair, the only piece of furniture at the centre of an otherwise empty and desolate room. She unsealed the envelope with the letter opener she had grabbed from the library and started to peruse it. For some reason, she had felt she needed to come up here to read it, here in the west wing, in the room that once was devoted to Lavinia. After a moment, her frowning face relaxed and she smiled - Mrs Monti was the sender and her words weren't adding anything to what Page already knew. To what she had known all along. Mrs Monti had ultimately foreseen his death - she wrote - but there was nothing she could have done at that stage other than to inform the others in order to intervene and prevent Lady Page's death from also happening. She could feel Mrs Monti's care from the tone of her lines, from the fine traits of her handwriting. What a gentle soul. She would call for her, someday. With a sigh, putting a hand on her hip to sustain her weight and the other on the armrest, she got up again and reached the mantelpiece. Unlike the windows, this was immaculate. She dusted it every single day. She carefully unfolded the letter, flattening it with her hands, and rested it on the mantelpiece. She looked up and smiled again, this time with glowing eyes - his portrait stood there, glorious, occupying the most important space in the empty room. Milord's room.

Peter had carefully avoided a detail all along, and so had Mr MacAllister. The two had exchanged a glance before leaving the post office, understanding each other immediately, while Mr Toulson, Mr Reede and Mrs Wood were starting to collect their belongings, awkwardly quiet. They both felt that it was better not to share this with the others, and to let the future have a say.

While giving the letter to Lady Page, the young postman had noticed that a new sparkle of life was dwelling inside her abused body, someone who one day would carry on the legacy of the place. Ivy and decay would never prevail at Lastsight Hill again.

ABOUT THE AUTHOR

Leni Remedios was born near Venice, Italy. She is a Birmingham-based writer of gothic and weird fiction as well as literary essays. Following her degree in Philosophy, completed at the Ca' Foscari University in Venice, she has collaborated with prominent philosophy and literature blog magazines such as *Critica Impura* and *Speechless*. *Milady's Room* is her first novel in English.